The Outdoor Girls at Rainbow Lake

Laura Lee Hope

The Outdoor Girls At Rainbow Lake

or

The Stirring Cruise of the Motor Boat Gem

by Laura Lee Hope

1913

CONTENTS

CHAPTER I

A GRAND SURPRISE

"Girls, I've got the grandest surprise for you!"

Betty Nelson crossed the velvety green lawn, and crowded into the hammock, slung between two apple trees, which were laden with green fruit. First she had motioned for Grace Ford to make room for her, and then sank beside her chum with a sigh of relief.

"Oh, it was so warm walking over!" she breathed. "And I did come too fast, I guess." She fanned herself with a filmy handkerchief.

"But the surprise?" Mollie Billette reminded Betty.

"I'm coming to it, my dear, but just let me get my breath. I didn't know I hurried so. Swing, Grace."

With a daintily shod foot—a foot slender and in keeping with her figure—Grace gave rather a languid push, and set the hammock to swaying in wider arcs.

Amy Stonington, who had not joined in the talk since the somewhat hurried arrival of Betty, strolled over to the hammock and began peering about in it—that is, in as much of it as the fluffy skirts of the two occupants would allow to be seen.

"I don't see it," she said in gentle tones—everything Amy did was gentle, and her disposition was always spoken of as "sweet" by her chums, though why such an inapt word is generally selected to describe what might better be designated as "natural" is beyond comprehension. "I don't see it," murmured Amy.

"What?" asked Grace, quickly.

"I guess she means that box of chocolates," murmured Mollie. "It's no use, Amy, for Grace finished the last of them long before Betty blew in on us—or should I say drifted? Really, it's too warm to do more than drift to-day."

"You finished the last of the candy yourself!" exclaimed Grace, with spirit. If Grace had one failing, or a weakness, it was for chocolates.

"I did not!" snapped Mollie. Her own failing was an occasional burst of temper. She had French blood in her veins—and not of French lilac shade, either, as Betty used to say. It was of no uncertain color—was Mollie's temper—at times.

"Yes, you did!" insisted Grace. "Don't you remember? It was one with a cherry inside, and we both wanted it, and — —"

"You got it!" declared Mollie. "If you say I took it — —"

"That's right, Grace, you did have it," said gentle Amy. "Don't you recall, you held it in one hand behind your back and told Billy to choose?" Billy was Mollie's "chummy" name.

"That's so," admitted Grace. "And Mollie didn't guess right. I beg your pardon, Mollie. It's so warm, and the prickly heat bothers me so that I can hardly think of anything but that I'm going in and get some talcum powder. I've got some of the loveliest scent—the Yamma-yamma flower from Japan."

"It sounds nice," murmured Betty. "But, girls — —"

"Excuse me," murmured Grace, making a struggle to arise from the hammock—never a graceful feat for girl or woman.

"Don't! You'll spill me!" screamed Betty, clutching at the yielding sides of the net. "Grace! There!"

There would have been a "spill" except that Amy caught the swaying hammock and held it until Grace managed, more or less "gracelessly," to get out.

"There's the empty box," she remarked, as it was disclosed where it had lain hidden between herself and Betty. "Not a crumb left, Amy, my dear. But I fancy I have a fresh box in the house, if Will hasn't found them. He's always—snooping, if you'll pardon my slang."

"I wasn't looking for candy," replied Amy. "It's my handkerchief—that new lace one; I fancied I left it in the hammock."

"Wait, I'll get up," said Betty. "Don't you dare let go, Amy. I don't see why I'm so foolish as to wear this tight skirt. We didn't bother with such style when we were off on our walking tour."

2

"Oh, blessed tour!" sighed Mollie. "I wish we could go on another one—to the North Pole," and she vigorously fanned herself with a magazine cover.

Betty rose, and Amy found what she was looking for. Grace walked slowly over the shaded lawn toward her house, at which the three chums had gathered this beautiful—if too warm—July day. Betty, Amy, and Mollie made a simultaneous dive for the hammock, and managed, all three, to squeeze into it, with Betty in the middle.

"Oh, dear!" she cried. "This is too much! Let me out, and you girls can have it to yourselves. Besides, I want to talk, and I can't do it sitting down very well."

"You used to," observed Amy, smoothing out her rather crumpled dress, and making dabs at her warm face with the newly discovered handkerchief.

"The kind of talking I'm going to do now calls for action—'business,' as the stage people call it," explained Betty. "I want to walk around and swing my arms. Besides, I can't properly do justice to the subject sitting down. Oh, girls, I've got the grandest surprise for you!" Her eyes sparkled and her cheeks glowed; she seemed electrified with some piece of news.

"That's what you said when you first came," spoke Mollie, "but we seemed to get off the track. Start over, Betty, that's a dear, and tell us all about it. Take that willow chair," and Billy pointed to an artistic green one that harmonized delightfully with the grass, and the gray bark of an apple tree against which it was drawn.

"No, I'm going to stand up," went on Betty. "Anyhow, I don't want to start until Grace comes back. I detest telling a thing over twice."

"If Grace can't find that box of chocolates she'll most likely run down to the store for another," said Amy.

"And that means we won't hear the surprise for ever so long," said Mollie. "Go on, Bet, tell us, and we'll retell it to Grace when she comes. That will get rid of your objection," and Mollie tucked back several locks of her pretty hair that had strayed loose when the vigorous hammock-action took place.

3

"No, I'd rather tell it to you all together," insisted Betty, with a shake of her head. "It wouldn't be fair to Grace to tell it to you two first. We'll wait."

"I'll go in and ask her to hurry," ventured Amy. She was always willing to do what she could to promote peace, harmony, and general good feeling. If ever anyone wanted anything done, Amy was generally the first to volunteer.

"There's no great hurry," said Betty, "though from the way I rushed over here you might think so. But really, it is the grandest thing! Oh, girls, such a time as may be ahead of us this summer!" and she pretended to hug herself in delight.

"Betty Nelson, you've just got to tell us!" insisted Mollie. "Look out, Amy, I'm going to get up."

Getting up from a hammock—or doing anything vigorous, for that matter—was always a serious business with quick Mollie. She generally warned her friends not to "stand too close."

"Never mind, here comes Grace," interrupted Amy. "Do sit still, Mollie; it's too warm to juggle—or is it jiggle?—around so."

"Make it wiggle," suggested Betty.

"Do hurry, Grace," called Mollie "We can't hear about the grand surprise until you get here, and we're both just dying to know what it is."

"I couldn't find my chocolates," said Grace, as she strolled gracefully up, making the most of her slender figure. "I just know Will took them. Isn't he horrid!"

"Never mind, did you bring the talcum?" asked Amy. "We can sprinkle it on green apples and pretend it's fruit juice."

"Don't you dare suggest such a thing when my little twins come along, as they're sure to do, sooner or later," spoke Mollie, referring to her brother and sister—Paul and Dora—or more often "Dodo," aged four.

They were "regular tykes," whatever that is. Mollie said so, and she ought to know. "If you gave them that idea," she went on, "we'd have them both in the hospital. However, they're not likely to come to-day."

"Why not?" asked Betty, for the twins had a habit of appearing most unexpectedly, and in the most out-of-the-way places.

"They're over at Aunt Kittie's for the day, and I told mamma I shouldn't mind if she kept them a week."

"Oh, the dears!" murmured Amy.

"You wouldn't say so if you saw how they upset my room yesterday. I like a little peace and quietness," exclaimed Mollie. "I love Paul and Dodo, but—and she shrugged her shoulders effectively, as only the French can.

"Here's the talcum," spoke Grace. "I'm sorry about the chocolates. Wait until I see Will," and she shook an imaginary brother.

"Never mind, dear, it's too hot for candies, anyhow," consoled Betty. "Pass the talcum," and she reached for the box that Mollie was then using. "It has the most delightful odor, Grace. Where did you get it?"

"It's a new sample lot Harrison's pharmacy got in. Mr. Harrison gave me a box to try, and said——"

"He wanted you to recommend it to your friends, I've no doubt," remarked Mollie.

"He didn't say so, but I haven't any hesitation in doing so. I just love it."

"It is nice," said Amy. "I'm going to get some the next time I go down-town."

The spicy scent of the perfumed talcum powder mingled with the odor of the grass, the trees, and the flowers, over which the bees were humming.

"Come, come, Betty!" exclaimed Mollie, vigorously, when shining noses had been rendered immune from the effects of the sun, "when do we hear that wonderful secret of yours?"

"Right away! Make yourselves comfortable. I'm going to walk about, and get the proper action to go with the words. Now, what did I do with that letter?" and she looked in her belt, up her sleeve, and in the folds of her waist.

"Gracious, I hope I haven't lost it!" she exclaimed, glancing about, anxiously.

"Was it only a letter?" asked Mollie, something of disappointment manifesting itself in her tones.

"*Only* a letter!" repeated Betty, with proper emphasis. "Well, I like the way you say that! It isn't a common letter, by any means."

"Is it from that queer Mr. Blackford, whose five hundred dollar bill we found when we were on our walking trip?" asked Amy, with strange recollections of that queer occurrence.

"No, it was from my uncle, Amos Marlin, a former sea captain," was the answer "A most quaint and delightful character, as you'll all say when you meet him."

"Then we are going to meet him?" interjected Grace, questioningly.

"Yes, he's coming to pay me a visit."

"Was that the grand surprise?" Amy wanted to know.

"Indeed not. Oh, there's the letter," and Betty caught up a piece of paper from underneath the hammock. "I'll read it to you. It's quite funny, and in it he says he's going to give me the grandest surprise that ever a girl had. It——"

"But *what* is the surprise itself?" inquired Mollie.

"Oh, he didn't say exactly," spoke Betty, smoothing out the letter. "But I know, from the way he writes, that it will be quite wonderful. Everything Uncle Amos does is wonderful. He's quite rich, and——"

"Hark!" exclaimed Amy.

A voice was calling:

"Miss Ford! Miss Ford!"

"Yes, Nellie, what is it?" asked Grace, as she saw a maid coming towards her, beckoning.

"Your brother wants you on the telephone, Miss Ford," answered the maid, "he says it's quite important, and he wants you to please hurry."

"Excuse me," flung back Grace, as she hurried off. "I'll be back in a minute. I hope he's going to confess where he put those chocolates."

CHAPTER II

AFTER THE PAPERS

"Hello, is this you, Will?"

"Yes, this is Grace. What did you do with my chocolates? The girls are here, and—Never mind about the chocolates? The idea! I like——. What's that? You want to go to the ball game? Will I do your errand for you? Yes, I'm listening. Go on!"

"It's this way, Sis," explained Will over the wire from a down-town drug store. "This morning dad told me to go over to grandmother's and get those papers. You know; the ones in that big property deal which has been hanging fire so long. Grandmother has the papers in her safe. The deal is to be closed to-day. I promised dad I'd go, but I forgot all about it, and now the fellows want me to go to the ball game with them.

"If you'll go over to grandmother's and get the papers I'll buy you a two-pound box of the best chocolates—honest, I will. And you can get the papers as well as I can. Grandmother expects one of the family over after them to-day, and she has them all ready.

"You can go just as well as I can—better, in fact, and dad won't care as long as he gets the papers. You're to take them to his office. Will you do it for me, Sis? Come on, now, be a sport, and say yes."

"But it's so hot, and Betty, Amy, and Mollie are here with me. I don't want to go all the way over to grandmother's after some tiresome old papers. Besides, it was your errand, anyhow."

"I know it, Sis, but I don't want to miss that game. It's going to be a dandy! Come on, go for me, that's a good fellow. I'll make it three pounds."

"No, I'm not going. Besides, it looks like a thunder storm."

"Say, Sis, will you go if I let you ride Prince?"

"Your new horse?" asked Grace, eagerly.

"Yes, you may ride Prince," came over the wire. Will was a good horseman, but for some time had to be content with rather an ordinary steed. Lately he had prevailed on his father to get him a new one, and Prince, a pure white animal, of great beauty, had been secured. It was gentle, but spirited, and had great speed. Grace rode well, but her mount did not suit her, and Mr. Ford did not want to get another just then. Will never allowed his sister to more than try Prince around the yard, but she was eager to go for a long canter with the noble animal. Now was the chance she had waited for so long.

"You must want to see that ball game awfully bad, to lend me Prince," said Grace.

"I do," answered Will. "But be careful of him. Don't let him have his head too much or he'll bolt. But there's not a mean streak in him."

"Oh, I know that—I can manage."

"Then you'll get those papers from grandmother for me, and take them to dad?"

"Yes, I guess so, though I don't like leaving the girls."

"Oh, you can explain it to them. And you can 'phone down for the chocolates and have them sent up. Charge them to me. The girls can chew on them until you come back. It won't take you long on Prince. And say, listen, Sis!"

"Yes, go on."

"Those papers are pretty valuable, dad said. There are other parties interested in this deal, and if they got hold of the documents it might make a lot of trouble."

"Trouble?"

"Yes. But there's not much chance of that. They don't even know where the papers are."

"All right, I'll get them. Have a good time at the game, Billy boy."

"I will, and look out for Prince. So long!" and Will hung up the receiver, while Grace over the private wire, telephoned to the groom to saddle Prince. Then she went out to tell her friends of her little trip.

And while she is doing this, I will interject a few words of explanation so that those who did not read the first volume of this series may have a better understanding of the characters and location of this story.

The first book was called "The Outdoor Girls of Deepdale; Or, Camping and Tramping for Fun and Health." In that is given an account of how the four chums set off to walk about two hundred miles in two weeks, stopping nights at the homes of various friends and relatives on the route. At the very outset they stumbled on the mystery of a five hundred dollar bill, and it was not until the end that the strange affair was cleared up most unexpectedly.

The four girls were Betty Nelson, a born leader, bright, vigorous and with more than her share of common sense. She was the daughter of Charles Nelson, a wealthy carpet manufacturer. Grace Ford, tall, willowly, and exceedingly pretty, was blessed with well-to-do parents. Mr. Ford being a lawyer of note, who handled many big cases. Mollie Billette, was just the opposite type from Grace. Mollie was almost always in action, Grace in repose. Mollie was dark, Grace fair. Mollie was quick-tempered—Grace very slow to arouse. Perhaps it was the French blood in Mollie—blood that showed even more plainly in her mother, a wealthy widow—that accounted for this. Or perhaps it was the mischievous twins—Dodo and Paul—whose antics so often annoyed their older sister, that caused Mollie to "flare up" at times.

Amy Stonington was concerned in a mystery that she hoped would some day be unraveled. For years she had believed that John and Sarah Stonington were her father and mother, but in the first book I related how she was given to understand differently.

It appears that, when she was a baby, Amy lived in a Western city. There came a flood, and she was picked up on some wreckage. There was a note pinned to her baby dress—or, rather an envelope that had contained a note, and this was addressed to Mrs. Stonington. Amy's mother was Mrs. Stonington's aunt, though the two had not seen each other in many years.

Whether Amy's parents perished in the flood, as seemed likely, or what became of them, was never known, nor was it known whether there were any other children. But Mr. Stonington, after the flood, was telegraphed for, and came to get Amy. He and his wife had kept her ever since, and shortly before this story opens they had told her of the mystery surrounding her. Of course it was a great shock to poor Amy, but she bore it bravely. She called Mr. and Mrs. Stonington "uncle" and "aunt" after that.

I described Deepdale and its surroundings in the previous book, so I will make no more than a passing reference to it here. Sufficient to say that the town nestled in a bend of the Argono River, a few miles above where that stream widened out into beautiful and picturesque Rainbow Lake. Then the river continued on its way again, increasing into quite a large body of water. On the river and lake plied many pleasure craft, and some built for trade, in which they competed with a railroad that connected with the main line to New York. In Rainbow Lake were a number of islands, the largest—Triangle—obviously so called, being quite a summer resort.

Our four girls lived near each other in fine residences, that of Mollie's mother being on the bank of the river. Deepdale was a thriving community, in the midst of a fertile farming section.

The summer sun glinted in alternate shadows and brilliant patches on Grace Ford as she hurried out to her friends on the lawn, after receiving the message from her brother Will.

"What happened?" asked Mollie, for it was evident from the expression on the face of the approaching girl that something out of the ordinary had been the import of the message.

"Oh, it was Will. He——"

"Did he 'fess up' about the chocolates?" inquired Mollie.

"No, but he's going to treat us to a three-pound box. I 'phoned down for them. They'll be here soon, and you girls can enjoy them while I'm gone."

"Gone!" echoed Betty, blankly. "Where are you going, pray tell?"

"Oh, Will forgot to do something father told him to, and he wants me to do it for him. Get some rather important papers from Grandmother Ford. I'm going to ride Prince. I wish you all could come. Will you be angry if I run away for a little while? I shan't be more than an hour."

"Angry? Of course not," said Amy, gently. "Besides, it's important; isn't it?"

"I imagine so, from what Will said. But he has the baseball fever, and there's no cure for it. So if you don't mind I'll just slip into my habit, and canter over. Oh, I just love Prince! He's the finest horse!"

"I'm afraid of horses," confessed Amy.

"I'm not!" declared Betty, who was fond of all sports, and who had fully earned her title of "Little Captain," which she was often called. "Some day I'm going to prevail on daddy to get me one."

"I should think you'd rather have an auto," spoke Mollie.

"I may, some day," murmured Betty. "But hurry along, Grace. It looks as though it might storm. We'll save some of the candy for you."

"You'd better!"

The chocolates came before Grace was ready to start after the papers, for she discovered a rent in her skirt and it had to be mended. Then, too, Prince proved a little more restive than had been anticipated, from not having been out in two days, and the groom suggested that he take the animal up and down the road on a sharp gallop to give the excess spirit a chance to be worked off. So Grace saw to it that she had at least part of her share of chocolates before she left.

"And I have just time to hear the rest about the grand surprise," she said to Betty, who had been turning and creasing in her hand the letter her uncle had written.

"I'm afraid I can't go as much into detail as I thought I could," confessed Betty. "But I'll read you the letter my old sea-captain uncle sent me. It begins: 'In port; longitude whatever you like, and latitude an ice cream soda.' Then he goes on:

"'Dear messmate. Years ago, when you first signed papers to voyage through life, when you weren't rated as an A. B., you used to have me spill sea-yarns for you. And you always said you were going to be a sailor, shiver my timbers, or something like that,—real sailor-like, so it sounded.

"'I never forgot this, and I always counted on taking you on a voyage with me. But your captain—that is to say your father—never would let me, and often the barometer went away down between him and me.

"'Howsomever, I haven't forgotten how you liked the water, nor how much you wanted a big ship of your own. You used to make me promise that if ever I could tow the *Flying Dutchman* into port that you could have it for a toy. And I promised.

"'Well, now I have the chance to get the *Flying Dutchman* for you, and I'm bringing it home, with sails furled so it won't get away. I'm going to give you a grand surprise soon, and you can pass it on to your friends. So if you let me luff along for a few more cable lengths I think I'll make port soon, and then we'll see what sort of a sailor you'll make. You may expect the surprise shortly.'

"That's all there is to it," concluded Betty, "and I've been puzzling my brains as to just what the surprise may be."

"He's going to take you on a voyage," said Amy.

"He's bought you some toy ship," was the opinion of Mollie.

"Oh, if he'd only bring a real boat that we could make real a trip in!" sighed Grace. "That would be—lovely!"

"Betty Nelson! Write to your uncle right away!" commanded Mollie, "and find out exactly what he means."

"I can't," sighed Betty. "He's traveling, and one never knows where he is. We'll just have to wait. Besides, he is so peculiar that he'd just as likely as not only puzzle me the more. We'll just have to wait; that's all."

"Well, if it should be some sort of a boat, even a big rowboat, we could have some fun," asserted Grace.

"Yes, for mine isn't much account," remarked Mollie, who owned a small skiff on the river.

"I was so excited and amused when I got uncle's letter," said Betty, "that I didn't know what to do. Mamma puzzled over it, but she couldn't make any more out of it than I could. So I decided to come over here."

"I'm glad you did," spoke Grace, holding up her long habit in one hand and delicately eating a chocolate from the other "There comes James with Prince. Oh, he's run him too hard!" she exclaimed as she noted the hard-breathing animal.

"Oh, no, Miss," said the groom, who heard her. "That was only a romp for him. He'll be much easier to handle now."

He gave Grace a hand to help her mount to the saddle, and adjusted the stirrups for her.

"Good-bye!" she called, as she cantered off. "Save some of the chocolates for me," and the others laughingly promised, as they went back to the shade, to rest in the hammock or lawn chairs.

CHAPTER III

THE RUNAWAY

Grace cantered along the pleasant country road on the back of Prince. The noble animal had lost some of his fiery eagerness to cover the whole earth in one jump, and now was mindful of snaffle and curb, the latter of which Grace always applied with gentle hand. Prince seemed to know this, for he behaved in such style as not to need the cruel gripping, which so many horsemen—and horsewomen too, for that matter, needlessly inflict.

"Oh, but it is glorious to ride!" exclaimed the girl, as she urged the animal into a gallop on a soft stretch of road beneath wonderful trees that interlaced their branches overhead. "Glorious—glorious!"

"I hope those papers are not so valuable that it would be an object for—for some one to try to take them away from me," she mused. Instinctively she glanced behind her, but the peaceful road was deserted save for the sunshine and shadows playing tag in the dust. Then Grace looked above. The sky was of rather a somber tint, that seemed to suggest a storm to come, and there was a sultriness and a silence, with so little wind that it might indicate a coming disturbance of the elements to restore the balance that now seemed so much on one side.

"But if any one tries to get them away from us, we—we'll just—run away; won't we, Prince?" and she patted the neck of the horse. Prince whinnied acquiescence.

"Grandmother will be surprised to see me," thought Grace, as she rode on. "But I'm glad I can do as well as Will in business matters. I hope papa won't be too severe with Will for not attending to this himself."

She passed a drinking trough—a great log hollowed out, into which poured a stream of limpid water coming from a distant hill through a rude wooden pipe. It dripped over the mossy green sides of the trough, and Prince stretched his muzzle eagerly toward it.

"Of course you shall have a drink!" exclaimed Grace, as she let him have his head. Then she felt thirsty herself, and looked about for something that would serve as a mounting block, in case she got down. She saw nothing near; but a ragged, barefooted, freckled-faced and snub-nosed urchin, coming along just then, divined her desire.

"Want a drink, lady?" he asked, smiling.

"Yes," answered Grace, "but I have no cup."

"I kin make ye one."

Straightway he fashioned a natural flagon from a leaf of the wild grape vine that grew nearby, piercing the leaf with its own stem so that it formed a cup out of which a Druid might have quaffed ambrosia.

"There's a cup," he said. "I allers makes 'em that way when I wants a drink." He filled it from the running water and held it up. Grace drank thirstily, and asked for more.

"And here is something for you," she said with a smile, as she passed down some chocolates she had slipped into a small pocket of her riding habit.

"Say, is it Christmas, or Fourth of July?" gasped the urchin as he accepted them. "Thanks, lady."

Grace again smiled down at him, and Prince, having dipped his muzzle into the cool water again, for very pleasure in having all he wanted, swung about and trotted on.

The distance was not long now, and Grace, noting the gathering clouds, was glad of it.

"I'm sure I don't want to be caught in a storm," she said. "This stuff shrinks so," and she glanced down at her velvet skirt. "I wouldn't have it made up again. I hope the storm doesn't spoil Will's ball game,"

She urged Prince to a faster pace, and, cantering along a quiet stretch of road, was soon at the house of Mr. Ford's mother.

"Why Grace!" exclaimed the elderly lady, "I expected Will to come over. Your father said——"

"I know, grandma, but Will—well, he is wild about baseball, and I said I'd come for him."

"That was good of you."

"Oh, no it wasn't. I don't deserve any praise. Chocolates and Prince—a big bribe, grandma."

"Oh, you young folks! Well, come in. Thomas will see to Prince."

"I can't stay long."

"No, I suppose not. Your father wanted these papers in a hurry. He would have come himself, but he had some matters to attend to. And, its being rather a family affair, he did not want to send one of his law clerks. Those young men tattle so."

"I wonder if they are any worse than girls, grandma?"

"Oh, much—much! But come in, and I will have Ellen make you a cup of tea. It is refreshing on a hot day. Then I will get you the papers. It is very warm."

"Yes, I think we will have a shower."

"Then I must not keep you. Is everyone well?"

"Yes. How have you been?"

"Oh, well enough for an old lady."

"Old, grandma? I only hope I look as nice as you when I get——"

"Now, my dear, no flattery. I had my share of that when I was younger, though I must say your grandfather knew how to turn a compliment to perfection. Ah, my dear, there are not many like him now-a-days. Not many!" and she sighed.

Tea was served in the quaint old dining room, for Mrs. Ford, though keeping up many old customs, had adopted some modern ones, and her house was perfection itself.

"I suppose your brother told you these papers were rather valuable; did he not?" asked Mrs. Ford a little later, as she brought Grace a rather bulky package.

"Yes, grandma."

"And if they should happen to fall into other hands it might make trouble—at least for a time."

"Yes. I will take good care of them."

"How can you carry them?"

"In the saddle. Will had pockets, made especially for his needs. They will fit nicely. I looked before starting out."

"Very good. Then I won't keep you. Trot along. It does look as though we would have a storm. I hope you get back before it breaks. I would ask you to stay, but I know your father is waiting for those papers."

"Yes, Will said he wanted them quickly. Oh, well, I think I can out-race the storm," and Grace laughed.

She found that she really would have to race when, a little later, out on the main road, the distant rumble of thunder was heard.

"Come, Prince!" she called. "We must see what we can do. Your best foot foremost, old fellow!" The horse whinnied in answer, and swung into an easy gallop that covered the ground well.

The clouds gathered thicker and faster. Now and then their black masses would be split by jagged flashes of lightning, that presaged the rumbling report of heaven's artillery which seemed drawing nearer to engage in the battle of the sky.

"Prince, we are going to get wet, I'm very much afraid," Grace exclaimed. "And yet—well, we'll try a little faster pace!"

She touched the animal lightly with the crop, and he fairly leaped into greater speed. But it was only too evident that they could not escape the storm. The clouds were more lowering now, and the bursts of thunder followed more quickly on the heels of the lightning flashes. Then came a few angry dashes of rain, as though to give sample of what was to follow.

"Come, Prince!" cried Grace.

Suddenly from behind there came another sound. It was the deep staccato of the exhaust of an automobile, with opened muffler. It was tearing along the road.

Grace glanced back and saw a low, dust-covered racing car, rakish and low-hung, swinging along. It was evident that the occupants— two young men—were putting on speed to get to some shelter before the storm broke in all its fury.

Prince jumped nervously and shied to one side at the sound of the on-coming car.

"Quiet, old fellow," said Grace, soothingly.

The car shot past her, and at the same moment Prince waltzed to one side, or else the car swerved, so that only by the narrowest margin was a terrible accident averted. Grace heard the men shout, and there was a wilder burst of the opened muffler. Then she felt a shock, and she knew that the machine had struck and grazed Prince.

She glanced down and saw a red streak on his off fore shoulder. He had been cut by some part of the car.

The next moment, as the racing auto swung out of sight around a bend in the road, Prince took the bit in his teeth and bolted. With all her strength Grace reined him in, but he was wildly frightened. She felt herself slipping from the saddle.

"Prince! Prince!" she cried, bracing herself in the stirrups, and gripping the reins with all her might. "Prince! Quiet, old fellow!"

But Prince was now beyond the reasoning power of any human voice. The thunder rumbled and crashed overhead. Grace, above it, could hear the whining decrease of the exhaust of the big car that had caused her steed to run away.

"Prince! Prince!" she pleaded.

He did not heed. Farther and farther she slipped from the saddle as his wild plunges threw her out of it. Then there came a crash that seemed to mark the height of the storm. A great light shone in front of Grace. Myriads of stars danced before her eyes.

She flashed towards a house. From it ran two little tots, and, even in that terror she recognized them as Dodo and Paul, the two Billette twins. They were visiting a relative who lived on this road, she dimly recalled hearing Mollie say. Evidently the children had run out in the storm. A nursemaid caught Paul, but Dodo eluded the girl, and ran straight for the road along which Grace was plunging.

"Go back! Go back!" screamed Grace. "Go back, Dodo!"

But Dodo came on. The next moment the child seemed to be beneath the feet of the maddened horse, which, a second later, slipped and fell, throwing Grace heavily. Her senses left her. All was black, and the rain pelted down while the lightning flashed and the thunder rumbled and roared.

CHAPTER IV

THE MISSING DOCUMENTS

"How do you feel now? Do you think you can drink a little of this?"

Faintly Grace heard these words, as though some one, miles away, was repeating them through a heavy fog. Myriads of bells seemed ringing in her ears, and her whole body felt as though made of lead. Then she became conscious of shooting pains. Her head ached, there was a roaring in it. This was followed by a delicious drowsiness.

"Try and take a little of this. The doctor does not think you are badly hurt. Fortunately the horse did not fall on you."

Again it seemed as though the voice came from the distant clouds.

Grace tried to think—to reason out where she was, and discover what had happened; but when she did, that same ringing of bells sounded in her ears, her head ached and she felt she was losing that much-to-be desired drowsiness.

"Try and take it."

She felt some one raise her head, supporting her shoulders. She struggled with herself, resolving not to give way to that lethargy. She opened her eyes with an effort, and looked about her in wonder. She was in a strange room, and a strange woman was bending over her, holding a glass of some pleasant-scented liquid.

"There, you have roused up, my dear, try to take this," said the woman, with a smile. "The doctor will be back to see you in a little while."

"The doctor," stammered Grace. "Am I hurt? What happened? Oh, I remember, Prince was frightened by the auto, and ran away. Where is he?" she asked in sudden terror, as a thought came to her.

"He got up and ran off after he fell with you," said the woman, as she held the glass for Grace to drink. "We had no time to try and catch him, for there were others to attend to."

"Oh, but Prince must be caught!" cried Grace, trying to rise from the couch on which she was lying, but finding it too much of an effort.

"He will be, my dear," said the woman. "Don't fret about the horse. He did not seem to be hurt."

Oh, it isn't so much Prince himself, though Will would feel very badly if anything happened to him. It is — —"

Then Grace recalled that to mention the papers in the saddle bag might not be wise, so she stopped.

"There now, don't worry, my dear," spoke the woman, soothingly. "Some one will catch the horse,"

"Oh, he must be caught!" cried Grace. "You say the doctor was here to see me?"

"Yes, we sent for one soon after a passing farmer carried you in here when you fell and fainted. You were lying out in the rain— insensible. We managed to get off your wet dress, and I just slipped this dressing gown of mine on you."

"You were very kind. I can't seem to think very clearly," and poor Grace put her hand to her head.

"Then don't try, my dear: You'll be all right in a little while. Just rest. I'll see if the doctor can come to you now."

"Why is he here—in the house—is some one else ill?" asked Grace, quickly.

"Yes, my dear. Poor little Dodo was knocked down by the horse, and we fear is badly hurt."

"Dodo?" and the voice of Grace fairly rang at the name.

"Yes, little Dora Billette. This is her aunt's house. She and her brother Paul are visiting here."

"Yes, yes! I know. They live near me in Deepdale. Their sister Mollie is one of my best friends. I am Grace Ford."

"Oh yes, I know you now. I thought I recognized your face. I have seen you at Mollie's house. I am a distant relative. But rest yourself now, and the doctor will come to you as soon as he can. He has to attend to Dodo first, the little dear!"

"Oh! Dodo, Dodo!" cried Grace, much affected. "You poor little darling, and to think that it was my fault! I must go to her. Mollie will never forgive me!"

She tried to rise.

"Lie still," commanded the woman, but gently. "It was not your fault. I saw it all. The twins persisted in running out in the storm. The girl could not stop them. Dodo got away and ran directly for the horse."

"Yes, I saw that. I thought she would be terribly hurt. Oh, to think it had to be I and Prince who did it!"

"It was not at all your fault. If anyone is to blame it is those autoists for going so fast, and passing you so closely. There was no excuse for that. The road was plenty wide enough and they scarcely stopped a moment after you went down, but hurried right on. They should be arrested!"

"Oh, but poor Dodo! poor Dodo!" murmured Grace. "Is she much hurt?"

"The doctor is not sure. He is afraid of internal injuries, and there seems to be something the matter with one of her legs. But we are hoping for the best. Here, take some more of this; the doctor left it for you."

Grace was feeling easier now. Gradually it all came back to her; how she had raced to get home before the storm broke—the pursuing auto, the injured horse and then the heavy fall. She had no recollection of the passing farmer carrying her into the house.

The doctor came into the room.

"Well, how are we coming on?" he asked, cheerfully. "Ah, we have roused up I see," he went on, as he noted Grace sitting up. "I guess it is nothing serious after all. Just a bump on the head; eh?" and he smiled genially, as he took her hand.

"Yes, I feel pretty well, except that my head aches," said Grace, rather wanly.

"I don't blame it. With that fall they say you got it is a wonder you have any head left," and he put out his hand to feel her pulse, nodding in a satisfied sort of way.

"How—how is little Dodo?" faltered Grace.

Dr. Morrison did not answer at once. He seemed to be studying Grace.

"How is she—much hurt?" Grace asked again.

"Well, we will hope for the best," he answered as cheerfully as he could. "I can't say for sure, but her left leg isn't in the shape I'd like to see it. I am afraid the horse stepped on it. But there, don't worry. We will hope for the best."

"Little Dodo's sister is my best chum," explained Grace, the tears coming into her eyes. "Oh, when I saw her running toward Prince I thought I would faint! Poor little dear! I called to her, but she would not mind."

"That was the trouble," explained Mrs. Watson, who had been ministering to Grace, "she seemed just wild to get out in the rain."

"Well, it may yet come out all right," said Dr. Morrison, "but it is not going to be easy. I don't believe you need me any more—er——"

He paused suggestively.

"Miss Ford is my name," Grace supplied.

"Ah, yes, I am glad to know you. Now I must go back to the little one."

"Could I see her?" asked Grace, impulsively.

"I had rather not—now."

Grace caught her breath convulsively. It was worse than she had feared—not to even see Dodo!

"But you can talk to Paul," went on the physician. "Probably it will do him good to meet a friend. He is rather upset. His aunt, Mrs. Carr, with whom the children were staying for a few days, has telephoned to Mrs. Billette about the accident. Word came back that Nellie—is that the name—the larger sister——"

24

"Mollie," said Grace.

"Well, then, Mollie is to come to take Paul home. We cannot move Dodo yet."

"Oh, is Mollie coming here?"

"Yes. You can arrange to go home with her if you like. I believe Mrs. Carr asked for a closed carriage."

"Then, I will go home with Mollie and Paul. Oh, will they ever forgive me?"

"It was not your fault at all!" insisted Mrs. Watson." I saw the whole thing. Please don't worry."

"No, you must not," said the physician. "Well, I will go back to my little patient," and he sighed, for even he was affected by Dodo's suffering.

Grace sought out Paul, who was with his aunt, whom Grace knew slightly. Mrs. Carr greeted her warmly, and put her arms about her in sympathy. Paul looked up at the familiar face and asked:

"Oo dot any tandy?"

"No, dear," said Grace, gently, "but I'll get you some soon. Mollie will bring some, perhaps."

With this promise Paul was content, and Mrs. Carr left him with Grace.

Poor Grace! With all the whirl that her head was in, feeling as wretched as she did, one thought was uppermost in her mind—the papers in the saddlebag. So much might happen to the valuable documents that were needed now—this very instant, perhaps—by her father. She almost wanted to go out in the storm and search for Prince.

"But perhaps he ran straight home to the stable," she reasoned. "In that case it will be all right, if only they think to go out and get them from the saddle, and take them to papa. Oh, if only Will were home from that ball game. What can I do? The telephone! They will be worried when they see Prince come home, cut, and will think I am badly hurt. I must let them know at once."

Mrs. Carr took her unexpected guest to the telephone, and Grace was soon talking to her mother.

"Don't worry, Momsey," she said. "Prince ran away with me—an auto hit him—now don't faint, I am all right. I'm at Mollie's Aunt Kittie's. Poor Dodo is hurt, I'll tell you about that later. But, listen. Go out to the stable—I suppose Prince ran there: Get those papers from the saddle, and send them to papa at once. Grandma's papers. They are very important. What? Prince has not come home? Oh, what can have become of him? Those missing papers! Oh, telephone to papa at once! He must do something," and Grace let the receiver fall from her nerveless hand as she looked out into the storm. The rain, after a long dry spell, was coming down furiously.

CHAPTER V

THE GEM

Grace and Mollie were riding home in the carriage that had been sent to bring Mrs. Billette to the home of her relative, for the anxious mother, on hearing that Dodo could not be moved, had come to look after the injured child. Paul went home with his sister. He was munching contentedly on some candy, and all thought of the recent accident and scare had vanished in the present small and sweet happiness.

"Oh, it must have been perfectly dreadful, Grace," said Mollie, sympathetically. "Perfectly terrible!"

"It was! And are you sure you don't feel resentful toward me?"

"The idea! Certainly not. It was poor Dodo's fault, in a way; but I blame those motorists more than anyone else. They should be found."

"They certainly made a lot of trouble," admitted Grace. "But I would rather find Prince than them. I wonder where he could have run to?"

"Oh, probably not far, after he got over being frightened. Doubtless you'll hear of his being found, and then you can send for him, and recover the papers."

"If only the saddle doesn't come off, and get lost," said Grace. "That would be dreadful, for there would be no telling where to look for it."

"Most likely it would be along some road. Prince would probably keep to the highways, and if the girth should break and the saddle come off it would be seen. Then, by the papers in the pockets, persons could tell to whom it belonged."

"That is just it. Papa doesn't want anyone to see those papers. Some of them have to be kept secret. Oh, I know he will feel dreadful about the loss, and so will Grandma! It was partly her property that was involved in the transaction."

"But they can't blame you."

27

"I hope not. I'll never be forgiven by Will for letting Prince throw me and run away, though. He'll never let me take him again."

"It was partly Will's fault for not doing the errand himself," declared Mollie, with energy. "Then this might not have happened. Of course I don't mean," she added hastily, "that I blame him in the least for what happened to Dodo. But I mean the papers might not have been lost, for he would likely have carried them in his coat pocket, and not in the saddle."

"That is what I should have done, I suppose," spoke Grace with a sigh. "But my riding habit had no pocket large enough. Oh, dear! I'm afraid it will be spoiled by the mud and rain," for she had left it at Mrs. Carr's and had borrowed a dress to wear home in the carriage, a dress that was rather incongruous in conjunction with her riding boots and derby hat.

"It can be cleaned," consoled Mollie. "No, Paul, not another bit of candy. Don't give him any, Grace. He'll be ill, and as I'll have to look after him when mamma is away I don't want to have it any harder than necessary."

"Me ikes tandy," remarked Paul. "Dodo ikes tandy too. Why not Dodo come wif us?" His big eyes looked appealing at his sister, and her own filled with tears, while those of Grace were not dry.

"Poor little Dodo," said Mollie. Then with a smile, and brushing away her tears, she spoke more brightly, "but we must not be gloomy. I just *know* she will be all right."

"I shall never cease praying that she will," spoke Grace, softly.

They were splashing home through the mud. The rain was still coming down, but not so hard. The long, dry spell had broken, and it seemed that a continued wet one had set in.

Grace was left at her house, where she found Amy and Betty ready to sympathize with her. Her father was there also, and Will. Both looked grave.

Seeing that family matters awaited discussion, Amy and Betty soon took their leave, after being assured that Grace was all right, except for a stiffness and a few cuts caused by the fall. A carriage took the two girls to their homes. Mollie had gone on with Paul.

"What will happen if we can't find the papers?" asked Grace of her father, when she had explained everything.

"Well, there will be a lot of trouble," he said, "and of course the whole matter will have to be held up. In the meanwhile, even if the other interests do not get the documents, they may make it unpleasant for us. I wish, Will, that you had done this errand yourself—not that I blame you Grace," he said quickly, "but Will knew how very important it was."

"I'm very sorry, Dad. I'll never cut business for a ball game again, and I'll do all I can to help out. I'm sure Prince will soon come home, though, and it will be all right. I'll go out to the stable now, and if he isn't there I'll saddle Toto and go hunting. I'll start from where the accident happened, and trace Prince. Lucky he's pure white, he'll show up well, even in the dark."

"No, I don't want you to do that," objected Mr. Ford. "You may go to the stable, if you like, but don't start any search until morning. In the meanwhile we may hear something, or he may come back. It's too bad a night to go out. But let this be a lesson to you, Will."

"I will; yes, sir. Poor little Sis, I can't tell you how sorry I am. Are you much hurt?" and Will laid his hand tenderly on her head. She winced, for he had touched a bruised place.

"Don't worry," she said, as brightly as she could. "I am all right, and the papers may be found. It is poor little Dodo I feel so badly about. She—she may be a cripple, the doctor says."

"No!" exclaimed Will, aghast.

"It seems terrible, but that is his opinion."

"Oh, they can do such wonderful things in surgery now a-days," said Mrs. Ford, "that I'm sure, in such a young child, there are many chances in her favor. Don't worry, daughter dear. Now you must go to bed, or you will be ill over this. Those motorists ought to be punished, if any one is."

"Yes," agreed Mr. Ford. "Now I must see what I can do to offset this loss. You don't suppose, do you Grace, that those men could have had any object in getting those papers away from you?"

"What do you mean?" asked Grace, in wonderment.

"I mean, did they seem to follow you—as if they had knowledge that the papers would be transferred to-day, and were determined to get them?"

"I don't think so, Daddy. I'm sure they didn't follow me. They just seemed to come out of the storm—trying to get away from it—as I was doing. I'm sure it was all an accident—just carelessness.

"Very likely. I was foolish to suggest it, but so much depends on those papers that I don't know just what to think. But there, Grace," as he kissed her, "you must rest yourself. I will think of a way out, I'm sure. Will, come with me. I may need you to make some memoranda while I telephone," and he and his son went to the library.

Morning did not see Prince in the stable, and all that day Will searched without result. Many had seen the white horse flying wildly past, but that was all. Some said the saddle was still on, others that it had come off. Mr. Ford was much exercised over the loss of the papers.

He did what he could to hold back the business, but there was a prospect of loss and considerable trouble if the documents were not eventually found. The opposing interests learned of the halt, and tried to take advantage of it. They were, however, only partly successful.

In the meanwhile, after several days had passed, Dodo grew well enough to be brought home. The chief injury was to her leg, and there was grave danger of it being permanently lame. As soon as she was in better condition it was decided to have a noted specialist treat her.

Prince remained missing, nor was there any report of the saddle being located, though Mr. Ford offered a liberal reward for that, or the return of the horse.

Betty had telephoned for her three friends. Her voice held in it the hint of pleasure and mystery both, but to all inquiries of what was wanted she returned only the answer:

"Come and see. I want you to meet some one."

It was two weeks after the accident, and, in a great measure, the bitter memories of it had passed. Dodo was doing as well as could be expected, and, save for a slight limp, Grace had fully recovered.

The three chums—"graces" Will called them—arrived at Betty's house at the same time. With sparkling eyes she led them into the parlor.

"But what is it?" whispered Amy.

"If it's a strange young man, I'm not going to go and meet him," said Mollie, with quick decision.

"It's a man, but not young, and I think you'll be glad to meet him," answered Betty.

Grace instinctively looked at her dress.

"Oh, you're all right!" cried Betty. Then she threw open the parlor door. "Here they are, Uncle Amos!" she cried, gaily, and the girls beheld a rather grizzled, elderly man, with tanned face and hands, and wrinkled cheeks, like an apple that has kept all winter, with the merriest blue eyes imaginable, and when he spoke there sounded the heartiest voice that could well fit into the rather small parlor.

"Avast there!" he cried, as he saw the girls. "So these are your consorts; eh, Bet? They do you proud! May I be keel-hauled if I've seen a prettier set of sails on a craft in a long while. It's good rigging—good rigging," and he glanced particularly at the dresses.

Betty presented her friends in turn, and Mr. Martin had something odd to say to each as he shook hands heartily.

"Uncle Amos has brought the—surprise," said Betty. "But even yet he won't tell me what it is."

"If I did it wouldn't be a surprise!" he protested. "But I'm all prepared to pilot you down to where she is. She's in the offing, all fitted for a cruise. All she needs is a captain and crew, and I think Bet

31

here will be the one, and you girls the other. I may ship as cook or cabin boy, if you'll have me, but that is as may be. Now, if you're ready we'll go down to the dock and see how the tide is."

"But we have no tide here, Uncle Amos," spoke Betty.

"What! No tide! What sort of a place is it without a tide? I'm disappointed, lass, disappointed!"

"We'll try and have one made for you," said Mollie, with a laugh.

"That's it! That's the way to talk. Salt water and a tide would make any place, even a desert—er—er—what is it I want to say, Bet?"

"I don't know, Uncle, unless that it would make the desert blossom like the rose."

"That's it—a rose. You luffed just at the right time. Well, ladies, all hands have been piped to quarters, so we'll start. It's nearly four bells, and I told the mate I'd be there by then. Let's start."

And start they did. On the way toward the river, whither Mr. Marlin insisted on leading the girls, Betty explained how her uncle had arrived unexpectedly that day, and had talked mysteriously about the surprise.

"It's a boat—I'm sure it is," said Mollie.

"Oh, he'd talk that same way about an automobile or an airship," said Betty. "He calls everything, 'she,' and if it was an auto he'd 'anchor' it near the river just to be close to the water he loves so much."

"What if it's an airship?" asked Amy.

"I shall—learn to run it!" declared Betty.

"Never!"

"Yes I shall."

"Let us hope it is but a rowboat then," sighed Amy.

They went out on the public dock in the Argono River. At the string piece was tied what the girls saw was one of the neatest motor boats that, as Will said afterward, "ever ate a gasoline sandwich."

There was a trunk cabin, an ample cockpit at the stern, a little cooking galley, a powerful motor, complete fittings and everything that the most exacting motor boat enthusiast could desire.

"There she is!" cried Mr. Marlin. "There's the surprise, Bet. I got her for you! I named her the *Gem*—for she is a gem. Aside from an ocean steamer there's no better boat built. I saw to it myself. I've been planning that for you for years. And there you are. The *Gem* is yours. I want you girls to take a cruise in her, and if you don't have a good time it will be your own fault. There's the *Gem* for you, Betty. Let's go aboard and see if that rascally mate has grub ready. There's the *Gem!*" and he led the way toward the beautiful boat. The girls simply gasped with delight, and Betty turned pale—at least Grace said so.

CHAPTER VI

READY FOR A CRUISE

"What a pretty cabin!" cried Mollie.

"And see the places to put things!" exclaimed Betty.

"Places to put things!" fairly snorted Mr. Marlin, or to give him his proper title, Captain Marlin. "Places! Huh! Lockers, young ladies! Lockers! That's where you *put* things. The aft starboard locker, the for'd port locker. You must learn sea lingo if you're to cruise in the *Gem*."

The girls were still aboard the new motor boat. They could not seem to leave it since Betty had been told that it was a gift from her uncle. They inspected every part, turned the wheel, daintily touched the shining motor, and even tried the bunks.

"There is room for five in the cabin," said Betty, looking about. "If we wanted to take another girl with us we could, when we go cruising."

"Or a chaperone," added Grace. "We may have to do that, you know."

"Well, we can," admitted Betty. "The question is, shall we go on a cruise?"

"Ask us!" exclaimed Mollie with a laugh. "Just ask us!"

"I do ask you," retorted the little captain of the *Gem*. "Girls, you are hereby invited to accompany me on a cruise to go—Oh, where can we go?"

"To Rainbow Lake, of course," said Grace, promptly. "We can go down the river into the lake, motor about it, go out into the lower river if we want to, camp on an island or two, if we like, and have a general good time."

"That's the way to talk!" cried Captain Marlin. "And I'll come with you part of the time. There's some extra bunks back here maybe you didn't see," and he showed them three folding ones in the cockpit back of the trunk cabin, where awnings could be stretched in stormy weather, enclosing that part of the craft.

"But what makes the boat go?" asked gentle Amy.

"The motor makes it 'mote,'" spoke Betty. "It's up in front; isn't it, Uncle Amos?"

"Up in front! There you go again, Bet. Up in front! You mean for'ard; up for'ard!"

"That's right, Uncle, I forgot. Come, we'll show these girls where the motor is," and she led the way to where the machinery was enclosed in a large compartment in the bow, close by hinged wing-covers.

The motor, one of three cylinders, was a self-starter, but by means of a crank and chain could be started from the steering platform, just aft of the trunk cabin, in case of emergency. There was a clutch, so that the motor could be set in motion without starting the boat, until the clutch, set for forward or reverse motion, had been adjusted, just as the motor of an automobile can be allowed to run without the car itself moving.

"And what a dear little stove in the kitchen!" exclaimed Betty, as the girls looked in the cooking compartment—it was not much more than a compartment.

"Kitchen!" cried Captain Marlin. "That isn't a kitchen!"

"What is it?" Amy wanted to know.

"The galley, lass, the galley. That's where we cook aboard a ship, in the galley. There's an alcohol and oil stove combined. You can have chafing dish parties—is that what you call them? and he laughed.

"That's right, Uncle," cried Betty. "And see the—what are we supposed to call these?" and she pointed to pots, pans, dishes and other utensils that hung around the galley.

"Oh, call 'em galley truck, that's as good a name as any," said the old captain. "Do you like this, Bet?"

"Like it, Uncle Amos! It's the dearest little boat in the world. I don't deserve it. You are so good to get it for me, and it was such a surprise."

"Yes, I calculated it would be a surprise, all right. But I didn't forget that you always wanted to be a sailor, and so when I got the chance, I made up my mind I'd get you something worth while before I got sent to Davy Jones' locker."

"Where is that?" asked Amy, innocently.

"Oh, he means before he got drowned, or something like that," explained Betty. "Oh, Uncle Amos, you're a dear!" and she kissed him, somewhat to his confusion.

"So I got a man to build this boat to suit my ideas," went on the old seaman. "It's equipped for salt water, if so be you should ever want to take a trip to sea."

"Never!" cried Mollie.

"Well, you never can tell," he said sagely. "After she was finished I had him ship her here, and then I got her into the water. I will say, that, for her size, she is a sweet little craft. And I hope you'll like her, Bet."

"Like her! Who could help it? Uncle you're a ——"

"No more kissing, Bet. I'm too old for that."

"The idea! Oh, girls, aren't the bunks too cute for anything!" and Betty sat down on one.

"And the dining room—may I call it that?" Grace timidly asked of the captain.

"Well, saloon is a better word, but let it go," he murmured. "Now, what do you say to a little run down the river? It will give you an idea of how to handle her."

"Oh, how lovely!" cried Betty. "Let's go, girls."

"That man is from the firm that built the craft," went on the former sailor. "He'll show you all the wrinkles," and he motioned to a man standing near.

Lines were cast off, the motor started, the clutch thrown in and then, with Captain Betty at the wheel, her uncle standing near to instruct her, the *Gem* started down the stream, attracting not a little attention.

"This is a sea wheel," explained the captain. "That is, you turn it the opposite way to what you want the boat to go. I wouldn't have a land-lubber's wheel on any boat I built. So don't forget, Bet, your boat shifts opposite to the way you turn the wheel."

"I'll remember, Uncle."

With dancing eyes and flushed faces, the girls sat in the cockpit back, or "aft," of the trunk cabin, and watched Betty steer. She did very well, for she had had some practice in a small motor boat the girls occasionally hired.

"Oh, I couldn't have had anything in the world I wanted more than this!" she cried to her uncle. "It is just great!"

"And you think you girls will go for a cruise?"

"I am sure we will, and as soon as we can. It will be the very thing for the hot summer."

"Wouldn't Will just love this?" sighed Grace.

"Perhaps Betty will invite him and Allen Washburn and Percy Falconer to come along on a trip or two," said Mollie, with a wink at her chums as she mentioned Percy's name. The latter was a foppish young man about town, who tried to be friendly with Betty; but she would have none of him.

"Never Percy!" she declared. "I'll ask Will, of course, and Frank Haley, but——"

"Not Allen?" inquired Amy, mischievously, for it was no great secret that Betty really liked Allen, a young law student, and that he was rather attentive to her.

"Which way shall I steer to pass that boat, Uncle?" asked Betty, to change a subject that was getting too personal.

"Port," he answered briefly.

"And that is——" she hesitated.

"The left," he answered quickly. "It's easy if you think that the letter L comes before the letter P and that L is the beginning of left. Port means left, always."

"I'm sure it's easy to say left and right," commented Grace, who was eating a chocolate.

"Hum!" exclaimed the old captain, disapprovingly.

The *Gem* proved worthy of her name. The girls made a little trip about the river, and then Captain Marlin, on learning that there was a boat house and dock on the property of Mollie's mother, steered the craft there, where it would be tied up until the girls started on their cruise.

And that they would cruise was fully decided on in the next few days. Now that the great surprise was known, plans were made to spend some time on the lake and river in the new craft.

The wonder and delight of it grew. Each day the girls discovered something different about Betty's boat. It was most complete, and practical. The boys were in transports over it, and when Will and his chum Frank Haley were allowed to steer they could not talk enough about it.

Preparations for the cruise went on apace. Captain Marlin oversaw them at odd times, for he was in business, and made trips between New York and Deepdale.

In the meanwhile Grace fully recovered from the runaway accident. Not so poor Dodo, however, and it was feared that the little girl would have to be operated on.

"When?" asked Betty, thinking that this would spoil Mollie's trip.

"Oh, not for some time," was the answer. "They are going to try everything else first."

Some of the mothers arranged to go along on part of the cruises, and other married ladies volunteered for the remaining days, so the girls would be properly chaperoned. Then began the final preparations.

"And if you see anything of Prince on your wanderings, don't fail to catch him," begged Will, a few nights before the day set for the start.

"We will," promised Grace.

The telephone rang—they were all at Grace's house. She answered.

"Yes, yes. This is Mr. Ford's residence. What's that—you have a stray white horse? Oh, Will, maybe it's Prince!" and she turned eagerly to her brother. "A man from Randall's livery stable is on the wire. He says they have a white horse that was just brought in. A farmer says he found him wandering about the country. Hurry down there!"

CHAPTER VII

STOWAWAYS

"Then he isn't your horse, Will?" It was Mr. Randall, the livery stable keeper who asked this question as Grace's brother critically inspected an animal that was led out for view in the stable.

"No, that isn't Prince," was the answer. "He looks enough like him, though, to be his brother. I'm much obliged for calling me up."

Will had hastened down after the receipt of the message Grace had taken over the telephone, for Randall's, as had all livery stables in the vicinity, had been notified to be on the lookout for the strangely missing animal, who might be wandering about the country carrying valuable documents in the saddle pocket.

"Two young fellows drove in here with this horse, and asked if they could put him up for a while," went on the livery man. "I didn't like the way they acted, but I didn't see how they could do me any harm, so I said they could. Then I got to thinking about your horse, and I called up. I'm sorry to disappoint you."

"I'm sorry myself, Mr. Randall. I can't imagine where Prince can be."

"Oh, some one has him, you may be sure of that. A valuable horse like that wouldn't go long without an owner. Maybe some one has changed his color—dyed him, you know. That has been done. Of course the dye doesn't last forever, but in this case it might hold long enough for the excitement to subside."

"Well, if they'll send back the papers, they can keep the horse, as much as I like Prince," Spoke Will, as he started home to tell his sister and the girls the details of the unsuccessful trip. He had already briefly telephoned to them of his disappointment.

"Oh, isn't it too bad!" cried Horace, as Will came back. "Do you really think, Will, that some one has Prince and the papers?"

"It looks so, Sis. Has dad said anything lately?"

"No, I believe the other side hasn't done anything, either, which might go to show that they haven't the papers. But it's all so uncertain. Well, girls," and she turned to her guests, "I guess we can finish talking about what we will wear."

"Which, means that I must become like a tree in Spring," sighed Will.

"How is that?" asked Amy. "Is it a riddle?"

"He means he must leave—that's an old one," mocked Mollie. "Any candy left, Grace?" and Mollie, who had been artistically posing on a divan, crossed the room to where Grace sat near a table strewn with books and papers, a box of chocolates occupying the place of honor.

"Of course there are some left," answered Grace.

"Which is a wonder!" exclaimed Will, as he hurried out of the room before his sister could properly punish him.

"Will we wear our sailor costumes all the while?" asked Betty, for the girls, as soon as the cruise in the *Gem* had been decided on, had had suits made on the sailor pattern, with some distinctive changes according to their own ideas. Betty had been informally named "Captain," a title with which she was already more or less familiar.

"Well, of course we'll wear our sailors—middy blouses and all—while we're aboard—ahem!" exclaimed Betty, with exaggerated emphasis. "Notice my sea terms," she directed.

"Oh, you are getting to be a regular sailor," said Mollie. "I've got a book home with a lot of sea words in. I'm going to learn them, and also how to tie sailor knots."

"Then maybe your shoe laces won't come undone so easily," challenged Grace, and she thrust out her own dainty shoe, and tapped the patent leather tip of Mollie's tie.

"It is not!" came indignantly from Billy.

"It is loose, and it may trip you," advised Amy, and Mollie, relinquishing a candy she had selected with care, bent over. The moment she did so Grace appropriated the Sweetmeat.

"As I said," went on Betty, "we can wear our sailor suits when aboard. When we go ashore we can wear our other dresses."

"I'm not going to take a lot of clothes," declared Grace, getting ready to defend herself against Mollie when the latter should have discovered the loss of the tidbit. "One reason we had such a good time on our 'hike,' was that we didn't have to bother with a lot of clothes. We shall enjoy ourselves much more, I think."

"And I agree with you, my dear," said Betty. "Besides, we haven't room for many things on the *Gem*. Not that I want to deprive you of anything," she added, quickly, for she realized her position as hostess. "But really, to be comfortable, we don't want to be crowded, and if we each take our smallest steamer trunk I think that will hold everything, and then we'll have so much more room. The trunks will go under the bunks very nicely."

"Then we'll agree to that," said Mollie. "Two sailor suits, so we can change; one nice shore dress, if we are asked anywhere, and one rough-and-ready suit for work — or play."

"Good!" cried Amy. "As for shoes — —"

"Who took my candy?" cried Mollie, discovering the loss of the one she had put down to tie her lace. "It was the only one in the box and — —"

Grace laughed, and thus acknowledged her guilt.

"I've got another box up stairs," she said. "I'll get it," which she proceeded to do.

"Grace, you'll ruin your digestion with so much sweet stuff," declared Betty, seriously. "Really you will."

"I suppose so, my dear; but really I can't seem to help it."

"As captain of the *Gem* I'm going to put you on short rations, as soon as our cruise begins," said Betty. "It will do you good."

"Perhaps it will," Grace admitted, with a sigh. "I'll be glad to have you do it. Now, is everything arranged for?"

"Well," answered Betty, "This is how it stands: We are to start on Tuesday, and motor down the river, taking our time. Aunt Kate will go with us for the first few days, and, as you know, we have arranged for other chaperones on the rest of the cruise. We will eat aboard, when we wish to, or go ashore for meals if it's more convenient. Of course we will sleep aboard, tying up wherever we can find the best place.

"I plan to get to Rainbow Lake about the second day, and we will spend a week or so on that, visiting the different points of interest — I'm talking like a guide book, I'm afraid," she apologized with a smile.

"That's all right — go on, Little Captain," said Amy.

"Well, then, I thought we might do a little camping on Triangle, or one of the other islands, say, for three or four days."

"Don't camp on Triangle," suggested Grace. "There are too many people there, and we can't be free. There'd always be a lot of curious ones about, looking at our boat, and our things, and all that."

"Very well, we can pick out some other island," agreed Betty. "You know there is to be a regatta, and water sports, on Rainbow Lake just about the time we get there, and we can take part, if we like."

"Do! And if we can get in a race we will!" cried Mollie, with sparkling eyes.

"Uncle Amos has promised to be with us some of the time," went on Betty. "And I suppose we will have to invite the boys occasionally, just for the day, you know."

"Oh, don't make too much of an effort," exclaimed Mollie. "Allen Washburn said he might be going abroad this summer, anyhow."

"Who said anything about him?" demanded Betty, with a blush.

"No one; but I can read — thoughts!" answered Mollie, helping herself to another candy.

"I meant Will and Frank," went on Betty. "They would like to come."

"I'm sure of it," murmured Grace — literally murmured — for she had a marshmallow chocolate between her white teeth.

"How about Percy Falconer?" asked Amy, mischievously. "I am sure he would wear a perfectly stunning — to use his own word — sailor suit."

"Don't you dare mention his name!" cried Betty. "I detest him."

"Let us have peace!" quoted Mollie. "Then it's all settled—we'll cruise and camp and——"

"Cruise again," finished Betty. "For we have two months, nearly, ahead of us; and we won't want to camp more than a week, perhaps. We can go into the lower river, below Rainbow Lake, too, I think. It is sometimes rough there, but the *Gem* is built for rough weather, Uncle Amos says."

The girls discussed further the coming trip and then, as each one had considerable to do still to get ready, they went gaily to their several homes.

Will came in later, looked moodily into an empty candy box, and exclaimed:

"You might have left a few, Sis."

"What! With four girls? Will, you expect too much."

"I wonder if I'll be disappointed in expecting a ride in Betty's boat?"

"No, we are going to be very kind and forgiving, and ask you and Frank. I believe Betty is planning it."

"Good for her. She's a brick! I wish, though, that we could clear up this business about the papers."

"So do I. Wasn't it unfortunate?"

"Yes. How is little Dodo coming on?"

"Not very well, I'm afraid," and Grace sighed. The injury to the child hung like a black shadow, over her. "The specialist is going to see her soon again. He has some hopes."

"That's good; cheer up, Sis! Come on down town and I'll blow you to a soda."

"'Blow'—such slang!"

"It's no worse than 'hike.'"

"I suppose not. Wait until I fix my hair."

"Good night!" gasped Will. "I don't want to wait an hour. I'm thirsty!"

"I won't be a minute."

"That's what they all say." But Grace was really not very long.

In answer to a telephone message next day the three chums assembled at Betty's house.

"I think we will go for a little trip all by ourselves on the river this afternoon," she said. "Every time so far Uncle Amos, or one of the boys, has been with us. We must learn to depend on ourselves."

"That is so," agreed Mollie. "It will be lovely, it is such a nice day."

"Just a little trip," went on Betty, "to see if we have forgotten anything of our instructions."

Just then a clock chimed out eight strokes, in four sections of two strokes each.

"Eight o'clock!" exclaimed Amy. "Your timepiece must be wrong, Betty. It's nearer noon than eight."

"That's eight bells—twelve o'clock," said the pretty hostess, with a laugh. "That's a new marine clock Uncle Amos gave me for the *Gem*. It keeps time just as it is done on shipboard."

"And when it's eight o'clock it's twelve," murmured Grace. "Do you have to do subtraction and addition every time the clock strikes?"

"No, you see, eight bells is the highest number. It is eight bells at eight o'clock, at four o'clock and at twelve—either at night, or in the daytime."

"Oh, I'm sure I'll never learn that," sighed Amy.

"It is very simple," explained Betty, "Now it is eight bells—twelve o'clock noon. At half-past twelve it will be one bell. Then half an hour later, it will be two bells—one o'clock. You see, every half hour is rung."

"Worse and worse!" protested Mollie. "What time is it at two o'clock?"

45

"Four bells," answered Betty, promptly. "Why, I thought four bells was four o'clock," spoke Grace.

"No, eight bells is four o'clock in the after-noon, and also four o'clock in the morning. Then it starts over again with one bell, which would be half-past four; two bells, five; three hells, half-past five, and — —"

"Oh, stop! stop! you make my head ache!" cried Grace, "Has anyone a chocolate cream?"

They all laughed.

"You'll soon understand it," said Betty.

"It's worse than remembering to turn the steering wheel the opposite way you want to go," objected Mollie. "But we are young—we may learn in time."

The *Gem* was all ready to start, and the girls, reaching Mollie's house, in the rear of which, at a river dock, the boat was tied, went aboard.

"Have you enough gasoline?" asked Amy, as she helped Betty loosen the mooring ropes.

"Yes, I telephoned for the man to fill the tank this morning. Look at the automatic gauge and see if it isn't registered," for there was a device on the boat that did away with the necessity of taking the top off the tank and putting a dry stick down, to ascertain how much of the fluid was on hand.

"Yes, it's full," replied Amy.

"Then here we go!" cried Betty, as the other girls shoved off from the dock, and the Little Captain pushed the automatic starter. With a throb and a roar the motor took up its staccato song of progress. When sufficiently away from the dock Betty let in the clutch, and the craft shot swiftly down the stream.

"Oh, this is glorious!" cried Mollie, as she stood beside Betty, the wind fanning her cheeks and blowing her hair in a halo about her face.

"Perfect!" echoed Amy. "And even Grace has forgotten to eat a chocolate for ten minutes."

"Oh, let me alone—I just want to enjoy this!" exclaimed the candy-loving maiden. They had been going along for some time, taking turns steering, saluting other craft by their whistle, and being saluted in turn.

"Let's go sit down on the stern lockers," proposed Grace after a while, the lockers being convertible into bunks on occasion. As the girls went aft, there came from the forward cabin a series of groans.

"What's that?" cried Mollie.

"Some one is in there!" added Grace, clinging to Amy.

Again a groan, and some suppressed laughter.

"There are stowaways aboard!" cried Betty. "Girls, we must put ashore at once and get an officer!" and she shifted the wheel.

CHAPTER VIII

A HINT OF GHOSTS

"Who can they be?"

"It sounds like more than one!"

"Anyhow, they can't get out!" It was Betty who said this last, Grace and Mollie having made the foregoing remarks. And Betty had no sooner detected the presence on the *Gem* of stowaways than she had pulled shut the sliding door leading into the trunk cabin, and had slid the hatch cover forward, fastening both with the hasps.

"They'll stay there until we get an officer," she explained. "Probably they are tramps!"

"Oh, Betty!" It was a startled trio who cried thus.

"Well, maybe only boys," admitted the Little Captain, as a concession. "They may have come aboard, intending to go off for a ride in my boat, and we came just in time. They hid themselves in there. That's what I think about it."

"And you are exactly right, Betty!" unexpectedly exclaimed a voice from behind the closed door. "That's exactly how it happened. We're sorry—we'll be good!"

"Dot any tandy?" came in childish accents from another of the stowaways.

The girls looked at one another in surprise. Then a light dawned on them.

"Don't have us arrested!" pleaded another voice, with laughter in it.

"That's Will!" cried Grace.

"And Frank Haley!" added Amy.

"And Paul!" spoke Mollie. "Little brother, are you in there?"

They listened for the answer.

"Ess, I'se here. Oo dot any tandy?"

"The boys put him up to that," whispered Grace.

Betty slid open the door, and there stood Will and Frank, with Paul between them. The boys looked sheepish—the child expectant.

"I ought to put you two in irons," spoke Betty, but with a smile. "I believe that is what is done with stowaways."

"Couldn't you ship us before the mast?" asked Will, with a chuckle. "That is the very latest manner of dealing with gentlemen who are unexpectedly carried off on a cruise."

"Unexpectedly?" asked Grace, with meaning.

"Certainly," went on her brother. "We just happened to come aboard to look over the boat, Frank and I. Then Paul wandered down here, and before we knew it we heard you coming. For a joke we hid under the bunks, and thought to give you a little scare. We didn't think you were going for a spin, but when you started we just made up our minds to remain hidden until you got far enough out so you wouldn't want to turn back. That's what stowaways always do," he concluded.

"I'm glad you do things as they ought to be done," remarked Betty, swinging the wheel over. She had changed her mind about going ashore after an officer.

"Dot any tandy?" asked Paul again.

"Do give him some, if you have any," begged Will. "We bribed him with the promise of some to keep quiet. Surely he has earned it."

"Here," said Grace, impulsively, as she extended some to the tot, who at once proceeded to get as much outside his face as into his mouth. Then she added rather sternly: "I don't think this was very nice of you, Will. Betty didn't invite you aboard."

"Oh, that's all right!" said Betty, good-naturedly. "I'm glad they're here now—let them stay. I'm so relieved to find they aren't horrid tramps. Besides, the motor may not—mote—and we'd need help— We will make them work their passage."

"Aye, aye, sir!" exclaimed Frank, pulling his front hair, sailor-fashion. "Shall we holystone the decks, or scrub the lee scuppers? You have but to command us!" and he bowed exaggeratedly.

"You may steer if you like," said Betty, graciously, and Frank and Will were both so eager for the coveted privilege that they had to draw lots to settle who should stand the first "trick."

For Betty's boat was a beauty, and the envy not only of Will and Frank, but of every other boy in Deepdale. So it is no wonder these two stowed themselves away for the chance of getting a ride in the fine craft.

"Let's go down as far as one of the lake islands," suggested Will, who was now at the wheel, his turn having come.

"Can we get back in time?" asked Betty. "The river is high now, after the rains, and there's quite a current."

"Oh, the *Gem* has speed and power enough to do it in style," declared Frank. "We'll guarantee to get you back in time for supper."

"All right," agreed the captain, who had gone into the cabin with the other girls.

"And perhaps we can pick out a good place to go camping," added Grace.

The boys directed the course of the boat, while the girls looked after Paul.

"We must stop at some place where there is a telephone," said Mollie, "and I'll send word to mamma that Paul is with me. She may be worried."

"Yes, do," suggested Betty. A little later the girls saw that the boys were approaching a dock, the main one of a small town just below Deepdale.

"Where are you going?" asked Grace of her brother.

"Going to tie up for a minute. Frank and I want to make amends for sneaking aboard, so we thought you'd like some soda. There's a grocery store here that keeps pretty good stuff."

"Oh, yes, I know Mr. Lagg!" exclaimed Mollie. "Barry Lagg is his name. He's real quaint and jolly."

"Then let's go ashore for the soda ourselves, and meet him," suggested Grace. "I am very thirsty. What is Mr. Lagg's special line of jollity?" she asked Mollie.

"Oh, he makes up little verses as he waits on you. You'll see," was Mollie's answer. I often stop in for a little something to eat when I am out rowing. He is a nice old gentleman, very polite, and he has lots of queer stories to tell."

"Has he dot any tandy?" inquired Paul, eagerly.

"Oh, you dear, of course he has!" cried his sister. "You are getting as bad as Grace," and she looked at her chum meaningly.

Will skillfully laid the *Gem* alongside the dock and soon the little party of young people were trooping up to the store, which was near the river front.

"Ah, good day to you all—good day, ladies and gentlemen, every one, and the little shaver too!" cried Mr. Lagg, with a bow as they entered his shop.

"What will you please to buy to-day?

 If it's coffee or tea, just walk this way,"

And, with this charming couplet Mr. Lagg started toward the rear of his store, where the aromatic odor of ground coffee indicated that he had spoken truly.

"We'd like some of your good soda," spoke Will.

"Ha, soda. I don't know that I have anything in the line of soda."

"No soda?" exclaimed Frank.

"I mean I haven't made up any poetry about that. I have about almost everything else in my store. Let me see—soda—soda——"

He seemed searching for a rhyme.

"Pagoda! Pagoda!" laughed Betty.

"That is it!" exclaimed Mr Lagg. "Thank you for the suggestion. Let me see, now. How would this do?

"If you wish to drink of Lagg's fine soda,

 Just take your seat in a Chinese pagoda!"

"Very good," complimented Will. "We'll dispense with the pagoda if you will dispense the soda."

"Ha! Good again! You are a punster, I see!"

Mr. Lagg laughed genially, and soon provided the party with bottles of deliciously cool soda, and straws through which to partake of it, glasses being voted too prosaic.

There came a protest from Paul, who was sharing the treat.

"I tan't dit no sody!" he cried. "It all bubbles up!"

"No wonder! You are blowing down your straw. Pull up on it, just as if you were whistling backwards," said Mollie.

"Whistling backwards is a distinctly new way of expressing it," commented Frank.

"I dot it!" cried the tot, as the level of his glass began to fall under his efforts—successful this time.

Then, having finished that, he fixed his big eyes on Mr. Lagg, and demanded:

"Oo dot any tandy?"

"Candy!" cried the eccentric store keeper. "Ha, I have a couplet about that.

"If you would feel both fine and dandy,

 Just buy a pound of Lagg's best candy!"

"That is irresistible!" exclaimed Will. "Trot out a pound of the most select."

"With pleasure," said Mr. Lagg.

Merrily the young people wandered about the store, the girls buying some notions and trinkets they thought they would need on the trip, for Mr. Lagg did a general business.

"What are all you folks doing around here?" asked the storekeeper, when he had waited on some other customers.

"Getting in practice for a cruise," answered Mollie. "Betty, here, is the proud possessor of a lovely motor boat, and we are going to Rainbow Lake soon."

"And camp on an island, too," added Amy. "I know I shall love that."

"Any particular island?" asked Mr. Lagg.

"Elm is a nice one," remarked Will "Why don't you girls try that? It isn't as far as Triangle, and it's nearly as large. It's wilder and prettier, too."

"Know anything about Elm Island, Mr. Lagg?" asked Frank, as he inspected some fishing tackle.

"Well, yes, I might say I do," and Mr. Lagg pursed up his lips.

"Is it a good place?"

"Oh, it's good all right, but — —" and he hesitated.

"What is the matter?" demanded Betty quickly. She thought she detected something strange in Mr. Lagg's manner.

"Why, the only thing about it is that it's haunted — there's a ghost there," and as he spoke the storekeeper slipped a generous slice of cheese on a cracker and munched it.

CHAPTER IX

OFF ON THE TRIP

The girls stared blankly at one another. The boys frankly winked at each other, clearly unbelieving.

"Haunted?" Betty finally gasped.

"A ghost?" echoed Amy, falteringly.

"What—what kind?" Grace stammered.

"Why, the usual kind, of course," declared Will. "A ghosty ghost, to be sure. White, with long waving arms, and clanking chains, and all the accessories."

"Stop it!" commanded his sister. "You'll scare Paul," for the child was looking at Will strangely.

"Oh, it's white all right," put in Mr. Lagg, "and some of the fishermen around here did say they heard clanking chains, but I don't take much stock in them. Tell me," he demanded, helping himself to another slice of cheese, "tell me why would anything as light as a ghost—for they're always supposed to float like an airship, you know—tell me why should they want to burden themselves with a lot of clanking chains—especially when a ghost is so thin that the chains would fall right through 'em, anyhow. I don't take no stock in that!"

"But what is this story?" asked Betty. "If we are thinking of camping on Elm Island, we do not want to be annoyed by some one playing pranks; do we, girls?"

"I should say not!" chorused the three.

"Well, of course I didn't see it myself," spoke Mr. Lagg, "but Hi Sneddecker, who stopped there to eat his supper one night when he went out to set his eel pots—Hi told me he seen something tall and white rushing around, and making a terrible noise in the bushes."

"I thought ghosts never made a noise," remarked Grace, languidly. She was beginning to believe now that it was only a poor attempt at a joke.

"Hi said this one did," went on Mr. Lagg, being too interested to quote verses now. "It was him as told me about the clanking chains," he went on, "but, as I said, I don't take no stock in that part."

"I guess Hi was telling one of his fish stories," commented Frank.

"Oh, Josh Whiteby seen it, too," said Mr. Lagg. He was enjoying the sensation he had created.

"Is he reliable?" asked Will.

"Well, he don't owe me as much as some," was the judicious answer. "Josh says he seen the white thing, but he didn't mention no chains. It was more like a 'swishing' sound he heard."

"Dot any more tandy?" asked Paul, and the laugh that followed in a measure relieved the nerves of the girls, for in spite of their almost entire disbelief in what they had heard, the talk bothered them a little.

"There are no such things as ghosts!" declared Betty, with excellent sense. "We are silly to even talk about them. Oh, there is something I want for my boat," and she pointed to a little brass lantern. "It will be just fine for going up on deck with," she proceeded. "Of course the electric lights, run by the storage battery, are all right, but we need a lantern like that. How much is it, Mr. Lagg?."

"That lantern to you

 Will cost—just two!"

"I'll take it," said Betty, promptly.

"Dollars—not cents," said the storekeeper, quickly. "I couldn't make a dollar rhyme in there, somehow or other," he added.

"You might say," spoke Will, "''Twill cost you two dollar, but don't make a holler.'"

"That isn't my style. My poetry is always correct," said Mr. Lagg, somewhat stiffly.

The lantern was wrapped up and the young people got ready to go down to the boat.

"Say, Mr. Lagg," asked Will, lingering a bit behind the others, "just how much is there in this ghost story, anyhow?"

"Just what I told you," was the answer. "There is something queer on that island."

"Then the girls will find out what it is!" declared Will, with conviction. "If they could find the man who lost the five hundred dollar bill, they're equal to laying the ghost of Elm Island. I'm not going to worry about them."

"Let's go down a little way farther and have a look at the haunted island," proposed Grace, when they were again on board the *Gem*.

"Have we time?" asked Betty.

"Lots," declared Will.

The motor boat was headed for the place. The island was of good size, well wooded, and the shore was lined with bushes. There were a few bungalows on it, but the season was not very good this year, and none of them had been rented. The girls half-planned to hire one to use as headquarters in case they camped on the island.

"It doesn't look very—ghostly," said Betty, as she surveyed it from the cockpit of her craft.

"No, it looks lovely," said Grace.

"Is the ghost going to keep us away?" asked Mollie.

"Never!" cried the Little Captain, vigorously.

"Hurray!" shouted Will, waving the boat's flag that he took from the after-socket.

They made a turn of the island, and started back up the river for Deepdale, reaching Mollie's dock without incident.

Busy days followed, for they were getting ready for the cruise. Uncle Amos went out with Betty and the girls several times to offer advice, and he declared that they were fast becoming good sailors.

"Of course not good enough for deep water," he made haste to qualify, "but all right for a river and a lake."

The girls were learning to tell time seaman fashion. Betty fairly lived aboard her new boat, her mother complained, but the Little Captain was not selfish—she invited many of her friends and acquaintances to take short trips with her. Among the girls she asked were Alice Jallow and Kittie Rossmore, the two who had acted rather meanly toward our friends just prior to the walking trip. But Alice was sincerely sorry for the anonymous letter she had written, giving a hint of the mystery surrounding Amy Stonington, and the girls had forgiven her.

Betty's Aunt Kate arrived. She was a middle-aged lady, but as fond of the great out-doors as the girls themselves. She was to chaperone them for a time.

The final preparations were made, the sailor suits were pronounced quite "chicken" by Will—he meant "chic," of course. Trunks had been packed, some provisions put aboard, and all was in readiness. Uncle Amos planned to meet the girls later, and see that all was going well. The boys were to be given a treat some time after Rainbow Lake was reached, word to be sent to them of this event.

"All aboard!" cried Betty on the morning of the start. It was a glorious, sunshiny day, quite warm, but there was a cool breeze on the river. "All aboard!"

"Oh, I just know I've forgotten something!" declared Grace,

"Your candy?" questioned Mollie.

"No, indeed. Don't be horrid!"

"I'm not. Only I thought——"

"I'm just tired of thinking!" returned Betty.

"Shall I cast off?" asked Will, who, with Frank, had come down to the dock to see the girls start.

"Don't you dare!" cried Mollie. "I'm sure I forgot to bring my——" She made a hurried search among her belongings. "No, I have it!" and she sighed in relief. She did not say what it was.

"All aboard!" cried Betty, giving three blasts on the compressed air whistle.

"Don't forget to send us word," begged Frank. "We want to join you on the lake."

"We'll remember," promised Betty, with a smile that showed her white, even teeth.

All was in readiness. Good-byes had been said to relatives and friends, and Mrs. Billette, holding Paul by the hand, had come down to the dock to bid farewell to her daughter and chums.

"Have a good time!" she wished them.

A maid hurried up to her, and said something in French.

"Oh, the doctor has come!" exclaimed Mollie's mother. "The doctor who is to look at Dodo—the specialist. Oh, I am so glad!"

"Shall I stay, mother?" cried Mollie, making a move as though to come ashore.

"No, dear; no! Go with your friends. I can send you word. You may call me by the telephone. Good-bye—good-bye!"

The *Gem* slowly dropped down the stream under the influence of the current and her own power, Betty having throttled down the motor that the farewell calls might be better heard. Mrs. Billette, waving her hand, hastened toward the house, the maid taking care of little Paul, whose last request was:

"Brin' me some tandy!"

CHAPTER X

ADRIFT

"Well, Captain Betty, what are your orders?" asked Amy, as the four girls, and Aunt Kate, stood grouped in the space aft of the trunk cabin, Betty being at the wheel, while the *Gem* moved slowly down the Argono River.

"Just make yourselves perfectly at home," answered Betty. "This trip is for fun and pleasure, and, as far as possible, we are to do just as we please. You don't mind; do you, Aunt Kate?"

"Not in the least, my dear, as long as you don't sink," and the chaperone smiled indulgently.

"This boat won't sink," declared Betty, with confidence. "It has water-tight compartments. Uncle Amos had them built purposely."

"It certainly is a beautiful boat—beautiful," murmured Mollie, looking about as she pulled and straightened her middy blouse. "And it was so good of you, Bet, to ask us on this cruise."

"Why, that's what the boat is for—for one's friends. We are all shipmates now."

"'Strike up a song, here comes a sailor,'" chanted Grace, rather indistinctly, for she was, as usual, eating a chocolate.

The girls, standing there on the little depressed deck, their hair tastefully arranged, topped by natty little caps, with their sailor suits of blue and white, presented a picture that more than one turned to look at. The *Gem* was near the shore, along which ran a main-traveled highway, and there seemed to be plenty of traffic this morning. Also, a number of boats were going up or down stream, some large, some small, and often the occupants turned to take a second look at the Outdoor Girls.

Certainly they had every appearance of living the life of the open, for they had been well tanned by the long walk they took, and that "berry-brown" was being added to now by the summer sun reflecting from the river.

"Is this as fast as you can go?" asked Mollie, as she looked over the side and noted that they were not much exceeding the current of the river.

"Indeed, no! Look!" cried Betty, as she released the throttle control that connected the gasoline supply with the motor. At once, as when the accelerator pedal of an auto is pressed, the engine hummed and throbbed, and a mass of foam appeared at the stern to show the presence of the whirling propeller.

"That's fine!" cried Grace, as Betty slowed down once more.

"I thought we'd take it easy," the Little Captain went on, "as we don't want to finish our cruise in one day, or even two. If I drove the *Gem* to the limit, we'd be in Rainbow Lake, and out of it, in too short a time. So I planned to go down the river slowly, stop at noon and go ashore for our lunch, go on slowly again, and tie up for the night."

"Then we're going to sleep aboard?" asked Grace.

"Of course! What would be the fun of having bunks if we didn't use them? Of course we'll sleep here."

"And stand watches—and all that sort of thing, the way your uncle told of it being done aboard ships?" Mollie wanted to know.

"There'll be no need of that," declared Betty. "But we can leave a light burning."

"To scare away sharks?" asked Amy, with a laugh.

"No, but if we didn't some one passing might think the boat deserted and—come aboard to take things."

"I hope they don't take us!" cried Mollie. "I'm going to hide my new bracelet," and she looked at the sparkling trinket on her wrist.

"Amy, want to steer?" asked Grace, after a while, and the girl of mystery agreed eagerly. But she nearly came to grief within a few minutes. A canoeist rather rashly crossed the bows of the *Gem* at no great distance.

"Port! Port!" cried Betty, suddenly, seeing the danger.

"Which is port—right or left? I've forgotten!" wailed Amy, helplessly.

"To the left! To the left!" answered Betty, springing forward. She was not in time to prevent Amy from turning the wheel to the left, which had the effect of swinging the boat to the right, and almost directly toward the canoeist, who shouted in alarm.

But by this time Betty had reached the wheel, and twirled it rapidly. She was only just in time, and the *Gem* fairly grazed the canoe, the wash from the propeller rocking it dangerously.

"We beg your pardon!" called Betty to the young man in the frail craft.

"That's all right," he said, pleasantly. "It was my own fault."

"Thank you," spoke Amy, gratefully. "Here, Bet, I don't want to steer any more."

"No, keep the wheel. You may as well learn, and I'll stand by you. No telling when you may have to steer all alone."

They stopped for lunch in a pretty little grove, and sat and talked for an hour afterward. Mollie hunted up a telephone and got into communication with her house. She came back looking rather sober.

"The specialist says Dodo will have to undergo an operation," she reported. Grace gasped, and the others looked worried.

"It isn't serious," continued Mollie, "and he says she will surely be better after it. But of course mamma feels dreadful about it."

"I should think so," observed Betty. "They never found out who those mean autoists were, did they?"

"No," answered Grace, "and we've never gotten a trace of Prince, or the missing papers. Papa is much worried."

"Well, let's talk about something more pleasant," suggested Betty. "Shall we start off again?"

"Might as well," agreed Grace. "And as it isn't far to that funny Mr. Lagg's store, let's stop and ——"

"Get some candy and poetry," sniped Amy, with a laugh.

"I was going to say hairpins, as I need them," spoke Grace, with a dignity that soon vanished, "but since you suggested chocolates, I'll get them as well."

They found Mr. Lagg smiling as usual.

"This fine and beautiful sunny day,

what will you have—oats or hay?"

Thus he greeted the girls, who laughingly declined anything in the line of fodder.

"Unless you could put some out as a bait for our horse Prince," spoke Grace. "It's the queerest thing where he can have gone."

"It is strange," admitted the genial storekeeper, who had heard the story from Will. "But if I hear of him I'll let you know. And, now what can I do for you?

"I've razors, soap and perfume rare,

To scent the balmy summer air,"

He bowed to the girls in turn.

"How about chewing gum?" asked Betty.

"Oh, would you?" asked Grace, in rather horrified tones.

"Certainly, aboard the boat where no one will see us."

"Gum, gum; chewing gum,

One and two is a small sum,"

Mr. Lagg thus quoted as he opened the showcase.

The girls made several purchases, and were treated to more of the storekeeper's amusing couplets. Then they started off again, having inquired for a good place at which to tie up for the night.

Dunkirk, on the western shore, was recommended by Mr. Lagg in a little rhyme, and then he waved to them from the end of his dock as the *Gem* was once more under way.

"Look out for that big steamer," cautioned Betty a little later, to Grace, who was steering.

"Why, I'm far enough off," answered Grace.

"You never can tell," responded the Little Captain, "for there is often a strong attraction between vessels on a body of water. Give it a wide berth, as Uncle Amos would say."

That Betty's advice was needed was made manifest a moment later, for the large steamer whistled sharply, which was an intimation to the smaller craft to veer off, and Grace shifted the wheel.

They reached Dunkirk without further incident, except that about a mile from it the motor developed some trouble. In vain Betty and the others poked about in the forward compartment trying to locate it, and they might not have succeeded had not a man, passing in a little one-cylindered boat, kindly stopped and discovered that one of the spark plug wires was loose. It was soon adjusted and the *Gem* proceeded.

"I'll always be on the lookout for that first, when there is any trouble after this," said Betty, as she thanked the stranger.

"Oh, that isn't the only kind of trouble that can develop in a motor," he assured her. But Betty well knew this herself.

They had passed Elm Island soon after leaving Mr. Lagg's store, but saw no sign of life on it. They intended to come back later on in their cruise and camp there, if they decided to carry out their original plans of living in a tent or bungalow.

"That is, if the ghost doesn't make it too unpleasant," remarked Betty.

They ate supper aboard the boat, cooking on the little galley stove. Then the work of getting ready for the night, washing the dishes, preparing the bunks, and so on, was divided among the five, though Aunt Kate wanted the girls to go ashore and let her attend to everything.

"We'll take a little walk ashore after we have everything ready," suggested Betty. The stroll along the river bank in the cool of the evening, while the colors of the glorious sunset were still in the sky, was most enjoyable.

"Gracious! A mosquito bit me!" exclaimed Grace, as she rubbed the back of her slim, white hand.

"That isn't a capital crime," laughed Mollie.

"No, but if there are mosquitoes here they will make life miserable for us to-night," Grace went on.

"I have citronella, and there are mosquito nettings over the bunks," said Betty. "Don't worry."

They went back to the boat, and the lanterns were lighted.

"Oh, doesn't it look too nice to sleep in!" exclaimed Amy, as they gazed into the little cabin, with its tastefully arranged berths.

"I'm tired enough to sleep on almost any thing," yawned Mollie. "Let's see who'll be the first to——"

"Not snore, I hope!" exclaimed Betty.

"Don't suggest such a thing," came from Amy. "We are none of us addicted to the luxury."

But, after all, tired as they were, no one felt like going to sleep, once they were prepared for it. They talked over the events of the day, got to laughing, and from laughing to almost hysterical giggling. But finally nature asserted herself, and all was quiet aboard the *Gem*, which had been moored to a private dock, just above the town.

It was Betty, rather a light sleeper, who awoke first, and she could not account at once for the peculiar motion. It was as though she was swinging in a hammock. She sat up, and peered about the dimly lighted cabin. Then the remembrance of where she was came to her.

"But—but!" she exclaimed. "We're adrift! We're floating down the river!"

She sprang from her berth and awakened Grace by shaking her.

CHAPTER XI

IN DANGER

"What is it? Oh, what has happened?"

Grace cried half hysterically as she saw Betty bending over her. The others awakened.

"Why, we're moving!" exclaimed Amy, in wonderment.

"What did you want to start off for, in the middle of the night?" Mollie asked, blinking the sleep from her eyes.

"I didn't," answered Betty quickly. "We're adrift! I don't know how it could have happened. You girls tied the boat, didn't you?"

"Of course," answered Grace. "I fastened both ropes myself."

"Never mind about that," broke in Aunt Kate. "I don't know much about boats, but if this one isn't being steered we may run into something."

"That's so!" cried Betty. "But I didn't want to go out on deck alone— slip your raincoats on, girls, and come with me! There may be—I mean some one may have set us adrift purposely!"

"Oh, don't say such things!" pleaded Grace, looking at the cabin ports as though a face might be peering in.

Quickly Betty and Mollie got into their long, dark coats, and without waiting for slippers reached the after deck. As they looked ahead they saw a bright light bearing directly for them. It was a white light, and on either side showed a gleam of red and green. Then a whistle blew.

"Oh, we're going to be run down!" cried Mollie. "A steamer is coming directly for us, Betty!"

"We won't be run down if we can get out of the way!" exclaimed Betty, sharply. "Push that button—the automatic, I mean—and start the motor. I'll steer," and Betty grasped the wheel with one hand, while with the other she pulled the signal cord, sending out a sharp blast that indicated her direction to the oncoming steamer would be to port. The steamer replied, indicating that she would take the same course. Evidently there was some misunderstanding.

"And we haven't our side lamps going!" cried Betty, in alarm, as she realized the danger. "Quick, girls, come up here!" she called to Grace and Amy. "One of you switch on the electric lamps. At least they can see us, then, and can avoid us. Oh, I don't know what to do! I never thought of this!"

A sudden glow told that Amy had found the storage battery switch, for the red and green lights now gleamed. Again the on-coming steamer whistled, sharply—interrogatively. Betty answered, but she was not sure she had given the right signal.

"Why don't you start the motor?" she called to Mollie.

"I can't! It doesn't seem to work."

"The switch is off!" exclaimed Grace, as she came out of the cabin. With a quick motion she shoved it over.

"How stupid of me!" cried Betty. "I should have seen to that first. Try again, Mollie!"

Again Mollie pressed the button of the self-starter, but there was no response. The *Gem* was still drifting, seemingly in the very path of the steamer.

"Why don't they change their course?" wailed Amy. "Can't they see we're not under control? We can't start! We can't start!" she cried at the top of her voice, hoping the other steersman would hear.

"The steamer can't get out of the channel—that's the reason!" gasped Betty. "I see now. It's too shallow for big boats except in certain places here. We must get out of her way—she can't get out of ours! Girls, we must start the motor!"

"Then try it with the crank, and let the automatic go," suggested Aunt Kate, practically. "Probably it's out of order. You must do something, girls!"

"Use the crank!" cried Betty, who was hobbling the wheel over as hard as she could, hoping the tug of the current would carry the *Gem* out of danger. But the craft hardly had steerage way on.

Mollie seized the crank, which, by means of a long shaft and sprocket chain, extending from the after cabin bulkhead to the flywheel, revolved that. She gave it a vigorous turn. There was no welcome response of throbbing explosions in the cylinders.

"Try again!" gasped Betty, "Oh, all of you try. I simply can't leave the wheel."

The steamer was now sending out a concert of sharp, staccato blasts. Plainly she was saying, loudly:

"Get out of my way! I have the right of the river! You must get out of my way! I can't avoid you!"

"Why don't they stop?" wailed Grace. "Then we wouldn't bump them so hard!"

As if in answer, there came echoing over the dark water the clang of the engine-room bell, that told half-speed ahead had been ordered. A moment later came the signal to stop the engines.

"Oh, if only Uncle Amos—or some of the boys—were here!" breathed Betty. "Girls, try once more!"

Together Mollie and Grace whirled the crank, and an instant later the motor started with a throb that shook the boat from stem to stern.

"There!" cried Betty. "Now I can avoid them."

She threw in the clutch, and as the *Gem* shot ahead she whistled to indicate her course. This time came the proper response, and a little later the motor boat shot past the towering sides of the river steamer. So near had a collision been that the girls could hear the complaining voice of the pilot of the large craft.

"What's the matter with you fellows?" the man cried, as he looked down on the girls. "Don't you know what you're doing?" Clearly he was angry.

"We got adrift, and the motor wouldn't start," cried Betty, in shrill tones.

"Pilot biscuit and puppy cakes!" cried the man. "It's a bunch of girls! No wonder they didn't know what to do!"

"We did—only we couldn't do it!" shouted Betty, not willing to have any aspersions cast on herself or her friends. "It was an accident!"

"All right; don't let it happen again," cried the steersman, in more kindly tones. And then the *Gem* slipped on down the river.

"What are we going to do?" asked Mollie, as Grace steered her boat.

"If we're going to stay out here I'm going to get dressed," declared Grace. "It's quite chilly."

Can you find your way back to the dock?" Aunt Kate inquired. "Can you do it, Betty?"

"I think so. We left a light on it, you know. I'll turn around and see if I can pick it out. Oh, but I'm all in a tremble!"

"I don't blame you—it was a narrow escape," said Mollie.

"I don't see how we could have gone adrift, unless some one cut the ropes," remarked Grace. "I'm sure I tied them tightly enough."

"They may have become frayed by rubbing," suggested Betty. "We'll look when we get a chance. What are you going to do, Amy?" for she was entering the cabin.

"I'm going to make some hot chocolate," Amy answered. "I think we need it."

"I'll help," spoke Aunt Kate. "That's a very sensible idea."

"I think that is the dock light," remarked Betty a little later, when the boat was headed up stream.

"Anyhow, we can't be very far from it," observed Grace. "Try that one," and she pointed to a gleam that came across the waters. "Then there's another just above."

The first light did not prove to be the one on the private dock where they had been tied up, but the second attempt to locate it was successful, and soon they were back where they had been before. Betty laid the *Gem* alongside the stringpiece, and Grace and Mollie, leaping out, soon had the boat fast. The ends of the ropes, which had been trailing from the deck cleats in the water, were found unfrayed.

"They must have come untied!" said Grace. "Oh, it was my fault. I thought I had mastered those knots, but I must have tied the wrong kind."

"Never mind," said Betty, gently.

CHAPTER XII

AT RAINBOW LAKE

Once the *Gem* was securely tied—and Betty now made sure of this—the tired and rather chilly girls adjourned to the cabin, and under the lights had the hot chocolate Aunt Kate and Amy had made.

"It's delicious," spoke Betty. "I feel so much better now."

"We must never let on to the boys that we came near running down a steamer," said Grace. "We'd never hear the last of it."

"But we didn't nearly run down a steamer—she came toward us," insisted Betty, not willing to have her seamanship brought into question. "If it had been any other boat, not drawing so much water, she could have steered out of the way. As it was we, not being under control, had the right of way."

"It wouldn't have done any good to have insisted on it," remarked Grace, drawlingly.

"No, especially as we couldn't hoist the signal to show that," went on Betty. "Uncle Amos told me there are signals for nearly everything that can happen at sea, but of course I never thought of such a thing as that we'd get adrift. I must be prepared next time."

"I can't understand about those knots," spoke Grace. "Where is that book?"

"What book?"

"The one showing how to tie different kinds of knots. I'm going to study up on the subject."

"Not to-night," objected Aunt Kate. "It's nearly morning as it is."

"Well, the first thing to-morrow, then," declared Grace. "I'm going to make up for my blunder."

"Oh, don't be distressed," consoled Betty. "Any of us might have made the same mistake. It was only an accident, Grace dear."

"Well, I seem fated to have accidents lately. There was poor little Dodo——"

"Not your fault at all!" exclaimed Mollie, promptly. "I'll not allow you to blame yourself for her accident. It was those motorists, if anyone, and I'm not sure they were altogether to blame. Anyhow, I'm sure Dodo will be cured after the operation."

"I hope so," murmured Grace.

The appetizing odor of bacon and eggs came from the little galley, mingled with the aromatic foretaste of coffee. Aunt Kate was busy inside. The girls were laughing out in the cabin, or on the lowered after-deck. It was the next morning—which makes all the difference in the world.

"I'm afraid we're going to have a shower today," observed Amy, musingly, as she looked up at the sky. A light fog hung over the river.

"Will you ever forget the awful shower that kept us in the deserted house all night?" asked Betty, as she arranged her hair. "I mean when we were on our walking trip," she added, looking for a ribbon that had floated, like a rose petal, under her shelf-dresser.

"Oh, we'll never get over that!" declared Mollie, who was industriously putting hairpins where they would be more serviceable. "And we couldn't imagine, for the longest time, why the house should be left all alone that way."

"Now I'm going to begin my lesson," announced Grace, who, having gotten herself ready for breakfast, took up the book showing how various sailor knots should be made. With a piece of twine she tied "figure-eights," now and then slipping into the "grannie" class; she made half-hitches, clove hitches, a running bowline, and various other combinations, until Amy declared that it made her head ache to look on.

The girls had breakfast, strolled about on shore for a little while, and then started off, intending to stop in Dunkirk, which town lay a little below them, to get some supplies, and replenish the oil and gasoline.

It was while Betty was bargaining for the latter necessaries for her motor in a garage near the river that she heard a hearty voice outside asking:

"Have you men seen anything of a trim little craft, manned by four pretty girls, in the offing? She'd be about two tons register, a rakish little motor boat, sailing under the name *Gem* and looking every inch of it. She ought to be here about high tide, stopping for sealed orders, and——"

"Uncle Amos!" cried Betty, hurrying to the garage door, as she recognized his voice. "Are you looking for us?"

"That's what I am, lass, and I struck the right harbor first thing; didn't I? Davy Jones couldn't be any more accurate! Well, how are you?"

"All right, Uncle. The girls are down in the boat at the dock," and she pointed. "The man is going to take down the oil and gasoline. Won't you come on a trip with us? We expect to make Rainbow Lake by night."

"Of course I'll come! That's why I drifted in here. I worked out your reckoning and I calculated that you'd be here about to-day, so I come by train, stayed over night, and here I am. What kind of a voyage did you have?"

"Very good—one little accident, that's all," and she told about getting adrift.

"Pshaw, now! That's too bad! I'll have to give you some lessons in mooring knots, I guess. It won't do to slip your cable in the middle of the night."

The girls were as glad to see Betty's uncle as he was to greet them, and soon, with plenty of supplies on board, and with the old sea captain at the wheel, which Betty graciously asked him to take, the *Gem* slipped down the river again.

At noon, when they tied up to go ashore in a pleasant grove for lunch, Mr. Marlin demonstrated how to tie so many different kinds of knots that the girls said they never could remember half of them. But most particularly he insisted on all of them learning how to tie a boat properly so it could not slip away.

Betty already knew this, and Mollie had a fairly good notion of it, but Grace admitted that, all along, she had been making a certain wrong turn which would cause the knot to slip under strain.

They motored down the river again, stopping at a small town to enable Mollie to go ashore and telephone home to learn the condition of little Dodo. There was nothing new to report, for the operation would not take place for some time yet.

Grace also called up to ask if anything had been heard of the missing horse and papers, but there was no good news. However, there was no bad news, Will, who talked to his sister, reporting that the interests opposed to their father had made no move to take advantage of the non-production of the documents.

"Have a good time, Sis," called Will over the wire. "Don't worry. It doesn't do any good, and it will spoil your cruise. Something may turn up any time. But it sure is queer how Prince can be away so long."

"It certainly is," agreed Grace.

"And so you expect to make Rainbow Lake by six bells?" asked Betty's uncle, as he paced up and down the rather restricted quarters of the deck.

"Yes, Uncle, by seven o'clock," answered Betty, who was at the wheel. "Six bells—six bells!" he exclaimed. "You must talk sea lingo on a boat, Bet."

"All right, Uncle—six bells."

"Where's your charts?" he asked, suddenly.

"Charts?"

"Yes, how are you sailing? Have you marked the course since last night and posted it? Where are your charts—your maps? How do you expect to make Rainbow Lake without some kind of charts? Are you going by dead reckoning?"

"Why, Uncle, all we have to do is to keep right on down the river, and it opens into Rainbow Lake. The lake is really a wide part of the river, you know. We don't need any charts."

"Don't need any charts? Have you heaved the lead to see how much water you've got?"

"Why, no," and she looked at him wonderingly.

"Well, well!" he exclaimed. "Oh, I forgot this isn't salt water. Well, I dare say you will stumble into the lake after some fashion—but it isn't seaman-like—it isn't seaman-like," and the old tar shook his grizzled head gloomily.

Betty smiled, and shifted her course a little to give a wide berth to some boys who were fishing. She did not want the propeller's wash to disturb them. They waved gratefully to her.

The sun was declining in the west, amid a bank of golden, olive and purple clouds, and a little breeze ruffled the water of the river. The stream was widening out now, and Betty remarked:

"We'll soon be in the lake now."

"The boat—not us, I hope," murmured Grace.

"Of course," assented Betty, "Won't you stay with us to-night, Uncle Amos?" she asked, as she opened the throttle a little wider, to get more speed. "You can have one of the rear—I mean after, bunks," she corrected, quickly.

"That's better," and he smiled. "No, I'll berth ashore, I guess. I've got to get back to town, anyhow. I just wanted to see how you girls were getting along."

The *Gem* was speeding up. They rounded a turn, and then the girls exclaimed:

"Rainbow Lake!"

In all its beauty this wide sheet of water lay before them. It was dotted with many pleasure craft, for vacation life was pulsing and throbbing in its summer heydey now. As the *Gem* came out on the broad expanse a natty little motor boat, long and slender, evidently built for speed, came racing straight toward the craft of the girls.

"Gracious, I hope we haven't violated any rules," murmured Betty, as she slowed down, for she caught a motion that indicated that the two young men in the boat wished to speak to her.

As they came nearer Grace uttered an exclamation.

"What is it?" asked Mollie.

"Those young men—in the boat. I'm sure they're the same two who were in the auto that made Prince run away! Oh, what shall I do?"

CHAPTER XIII

CRACKERS AND OLIVES

Betty grasped the situation, and acted quickly, as she always did in an emergency.

"Are you sure, Grace?" she asked. She could speak without fear of the men in the racing boat overhearing her, for they had thrown out their clutch, a moment later letting it slip into reverse, and the churning propeller, and the throb of the motor, made it impossible for them to hear what was said aboard the *Gem*. "Are you sure, Grace?" repeated Betty.

"Well, almost. Of course I only had a glimpse of them, but I have good cause to remember them."

"Don't say anything now, then," suggested Betty. "We will wait and see what they say. Later we may be able to make sure."

"All right," Grace agreed, looking intently at the two young men. They seemed nice enough, and were smiling in a pleasant, frank manner at the outdoor girls and Aunt Kate. The two boats were now slowly drifting side by side on Rainbow Lake, the motors of both stilled.

"I beg your pardon," said the darker complexioned of the two men, "my name is Stone, and this is my friend, Mr. Kennedy. We are on the regatta committee and we'd like to get as many entries for the water pageant as we can. Is your boat entered yet?"

He gazed from one girl to another, as though to ascertain who was in command of the newly arrived craft, which seemed to have attracted considerable attention, for a number of other boats were centering about her.

"We have just arrived," spoke Betty in her capacity as captain. "We are cruising about, and we haven't heard of any regatta or pageant, except a rumor that one was to be held some time this summer."

"Well, it's only been in process of arrangement for about a week," explained Mr. Stone. "It will be the first of its kind to be held on the lake, and we want it to be a success. Nearly all of the campers and summer cottagers, who have motor boats, have agreed to enter the parade, and also in the races. We'd like to enter you in both. We have different classes, handicapped according to speed, and your craft looks as though it could go some."

"It can," Betty admitted, while Grace was intently studying the faces of the two young men. The more she looked at them, the more convinced she was that they were the ones who had been in the auto.

"We saw you arrive," said Mr. Kennedy, who, Mollie said afterward, had a pleasant voice, "and we hurried over to get you down on the list the first thing."

"Don't disappoint us—say you'll enter!" urged Mr. Stone. "You don't know us, of course, but I have taken the liberty of introducing myself, If you are acquainted with any of the cottagers on the lake shore, or on Triangle Island, you can ask them about us."

"Oh, we are very glad you invited us," replied Betty, quickly. She did not want the young men to think that she resented anything. Besides, if what Grace thought about them was so, they would want a chance to inquire about the young men more closely, perhaps, than the young men themselves would care to be looked after. For Betty recalled what Grace had said—that her father had a faint idea that perhaps the motorists might have acted as they did purposely, to get possession of the papers.

"Then you'll enter?" asked Mr. Kennedy.

"We can't be sure," spoke Betty, who seemed to be doing all the talking. "Our plans are uncertain, we have no very definite ones, though. We intended merely to cruise about, and perhaps camp on one of the islands for a few days. But if we find we can, we will at least take part in the water pageant—that is, in the parade with the other boats."

"And we'd like you to be in the races," suggested Mr. Kennedy. "Your boat has very fine lines. What horse power have you?"

"It is rated twenty," answered Betty, promptly, proud that she had the knowledge at her tongue's end, "but it develops nearer twenty-five."

"Then you'd go in Class B." said Mr. Stone. "I will enter you, tentatively at least, for that race, and if you find you can't compete, no harm will be done. There are some very handsome prizes."

"Oh, do enter, Bet!" exclaimed Mollie in a whisper, for she was fond of sports of all kinds. "It will he such jolly fun!"

Betty looked at her aunt. Racing had not entered into their plans when they talked them over with the folks at home.

"I think you might; they seem very nice, and we can easily find out if other girls are to race," said Aunt Kate, in a low voice.

"You may enter my boat, then," said Betty, graciously.

"Thank you!" exclaimed Mr. Stone. "The *Gem* goes in, and her captain's name—?"

"Miss Nelson."

"Of—?" again he paused suggestively, pencil poised.

"Of Deepdale."

"Oh, yes, I have been there. I am sure you will not regret having decided to enter the regatta. Now if you would like to tie up for the night there are several good public docks near here. That one over there," and he pointed, "is used by very few other boats, and perhaps you would like it. Plenty of room, you know."

"Thank you," said Betty. "We shall go over there."

"I will send you a formal entry blank to-morrow," said Mr. Stone, as his companion started the motor, and a moment later they were rushing off in a smother of foam thrown up by the powerful racing craft.

"Well, what do you think of that?" gasped Mollie, when they had gone. "No sooner do we arrive than we are plunged into the midst of—er—the midst of—what is it I want to say?" She laughed and looked about for assistance.

"Better give it up," said Amy. "But what Grace said surprises me—about those two young men."

"Well, of course I can't be sure of it," said Grace, as all eyes were turned in her direction, "but the more I look at those two the more I really think they are the ones. I wonder if there isn't some way I could make sure?"

"Yes," said practical Betty, "there is. That is why I decided to enter the *Gem* in the regatta. It will give us a chance to do a little quiet investigating."

"But how?" inquired Grace, puzzled.

"Well, if we make some inquiries, and find out that they are all right to talk to—and they may be in spite of the mean way they acted toward you—why, then, we can question them, and gradually lead the talk around to autos, and racing, and storms, and all that. They'll probably let out something about having been caught in a storm once, and seeing a horse run away. Then we will be sure they are the same ones, and—well, I don't know what would be the best thing to do then, Grace."

"Grace had better notify her father or brother if she finds out these are the men," suggested Aunt Kate. "They would be the best ones to act after that."

"Surely," agreed Grace. "That's what I'll do. And now let's go over to the dock, and see about supper. I'm as hungry as a starved kitten."

"And with all the candy she's eaten since lunch!" exclaimed Mollie.

"I didn't eat much at all!" came promptly from Grace. "Did I, Amy?"

"I wasn't watching. Anyhow, I am hungry, too."

"I fancy we all are," spoke Betty. "Well, we will soon be there," and she started the motor, and swung the prow of the *Gem* over toward the dock.

There were one or two small open motor boats tied there, but they were not manned. The girls made sure of their cable fastenings, and soon the appetizing odor of cooking came from the small galley. The girls donned long aprons over their sailor costumes, and ate out on the open deck, for it was rather close in the cabin.

"It is as sultry as though there were going to be a storm," remarked Betty, looking up at the sky, which was taking on the tints of evening. "I am glad we're not going to be out on the lake to-night."

"Aren't we ever going to do any night cruising?" asked Mollie, who was a bit venturesome at times.

"Oh, of course. Why, the main water pageant takes place at night, one of those young men said, and we'll be in that. Only I'm just as glad we're tied up to-night," spoke Betty.

Near where they had docked was a little colony of summer cottages, and not far off was an amusement resort, including a moving picture show.

"Let's go, girls!" proposed Grace after supper, "We don't want to sit around all evening doing nothing. The boat will be safe; won't it, Betty?"

"Don't say 'it'—my boat is a lady—speak of her as such," laughed the Little Captain. "Yes, I think she will be safe. But I will see if there is a dock watchman, and if there is I'll engage him."

There proved to be one, who, for a small fee, would see that no unauthorized persons entered the *Gem*. Then the girls, attiring themselves in their "shore togs," as Betty expressed it, went to see the moving pictures.

"What will we do to-morrow?" asked Grace, as they came out, having had two hours of enjoyment.

"I was thinking of a little picnic ashore," answered Betty. "There are some lovely places on the banks of the lake, to say nothing of the several small islands. We can cruise about a bit, and then go ashore with our lunch. Or, if any of you have any other plan, don't hesitate to mention it. I want you girls to have a good time."

"As if we weren't having it, Little Captain!" cried Mollie with an impulsive embrace. "The picnic by all means, and please let's take plenty of crackers and olives."

"Talk about me eating candy," mocked Grace, "you are as bad on olives."

"Well, they're not so bad for one as candy."

"I don't know about that."

"Oh, don't argue!" begged quiet little Amy. "Let's talk about the picnic."

It was arranged that they should have an informal one, and the next morning, after an uneventful night—save that Grace awakened them all by declaring someone was coming aboard, when it proved to be only a frightened dog—the next morning they started off again, leaving word with the dock watchman, who did boat repairing, that they would be back late that afternoon.

They had made some inquiries, and decided to go ashore on Eel Island, so named from its long, narrow shape. There was a small dock there, which made it easy for the *Gem* to land her passengers, since she drew a little too much water to get right up to shore.

The girls cruised about Rainbow Lake, being saluted many times by other craft, the occupants of which seemed to admire Betty's fine boat. In turn she answered with the regulation three blasts of the air whistle. At several private docks, the property of wealthy cottagers, could be seen signs of preparation for the coming water carnival. The boat houses were being decorated, and in some cases elaborate schemes of ornamentation were under way for the boats themselves.

"It looks as though it would be nice," remarked Mollie.

"Yes, I think we shall enjoy it," agreed Betty.

They stopped at one cottage, occupied by a Mrs. Ralston, whom Betty knew slightly. Mrs. Ralston wanted the girls and Aunt Kate to stay to lunch, but they told of their picnic plans. They wanted to inquire about Mr. Stone and Mr. Kennedy, and they were all glad to learn that the two young men were held in the highest esteem, and were given a great deal of credit for their hard work in connection with the lake pageant.

"And to think they could be so unfeeling as to make Prince run away and cause all that trouble," observed Mollie, as they were again aboard the boat.

"Perhaps it was not they, or there may be some explanation of their conduct," suggested Betty. "We must not judge too hastily."

"That's Betty Nelson—all over," said Amy.

Eel Island proved to be an ideal picnic place, and there were one or two other parties on it when the girls arrived. They made the *Gem* secure, and struck off into the woods with their lunch baskets, Betty having removed a certain patented spark plug, without which the motor could not be started. It was not likely that anyone would be able to duplicate it and make off with the craft in their absence, so they felt it safe to leave the boat unguarded.

"Pass the olives, Grace my dear," requested Mollie, when they were seated on a grassy knoll under a big oak tree. "I have the crackers beside me. Now I am happy," and she munched the appetizing combination.

"Crackers and olives!" murmured Betty. "Our old schoolday feast. I haven't gotten over my love for them, either. Let them circulate, Mollie."

The girls were making merry with quip and jest when Grace, hearing a crackling of under brush, looked back along the path they had come. She started and exclaimed:

"Here come those two young men—Mr. Stone and Mr. Kennedy."

"Don't notice them," begged Amy, who was not much given to making new acquaintances.

"Too late! They see us—they're coming right toward us!" cried Grace, in some confusion.

CHAPTER XIV

THE REGATTA

The two young men came on, apparently with the object of speaking to the girls. Evidently they had purposely sought them out.

"Oh, it is Miss Nelson, and her friends from the *Gem*!" exclaimed Mr. Stone, which might indicate that he had expected to meet some other party of picnic lovers.

"I hope we are not intruding," said Mr. Kennedy, "but we want to borrow some salt, if you have any."

Betty looked at them curiously. Was this a subterfuge—a means to an acquaintance? Her manner stiffened a trifle, and she glanced at Aunt Kate.

"You see we came off on a little picnic like yourselves," explained Mr. Stone, "and Bob, here, forgot the salt."

"You told me you'd put it in yourself, Harry!" exclaimed the other, "and of course I thought you did."

"Well, be that as it may," said his friend, "we have no salt. We heard your voices over here and decided to be bold enough to ask for some. Do you remember us, Miss Nelson?"

"Oh, yes." Betty's manner softened. The explanation was sufficient. Clearly the young men had not resorted to this trick to scrape an acquaintance with the girls.

"Is there anything else you'd like?" asked impulsive Mollie. "Grace has plenty of candy, I think, and as for olives——" she tilted one empty bottle, and smiled. Mr. Kennedy smiled back in a frank manner. Betty decided that introductions would be in good form, since they had learned that the young men were "perfectly proper."

Names were exchanged, and Mr. Kennedy and his friend sat down on the grass. They did not seem in any special hurry about the salt, now that it was offered.

"We hope you haven't changed your minds about the race and regatta," spoke Mr. Stone, after some generalities had been exchanged. "By the way, I have the entry blanks for you," and he passed the papers to Betty, who accepted them with murmured thanks.

"We shall very likely enter both the pageant and the race," she said. "When do they take place?"

"The pageant will be held two nights hence. That will really open the carnival. The boats, decorated as suit the fancies of the owners, will form in line, and move about the lake, past the judges' stand. There will be prizes for the most beautifully decorated boat, the oddest, and also the worst, if you understand me. I mean by the last that some captains have decided to make their boats look like wrecks, striving after queer effects."

"I should not like that," said Betty, decidedly. "But if there is time, and we can do it, we might decorate?" and she looked at her chums questioningly.

"Surely," said Grace, and Mollie took the chance to whisper to her:

"Why don't you start some questions?"

"I will—if I get a chance," was the answer.

Betty was finding out more about the carnival when the start would be made, the course and other details. The races would take place the day after the boat parade.

"There will be canoe and rowing races, as well as tub and 'upset' events," said Mr. Stone. "We are also planning to have a swimming and diving contest the latter part of the regatta week, but I don't suppose you young ladies would care to enter that."

"We all swim, and we have our bathing suits," said Mollie, indefinitely.

"Mollie dives beautifully!" exclaimed Amy.

"I do not—that is, I'm not an expert at it," Mollie hastened to say. "But I love diving."

"Then why not enter?" asked Mr. Kennedy. "I am chairman of that committee. I'll put the names of you girls down, if you don't mind. It doesn't commit you to anything."

The girls had no formal objections.

"You are real out-door girls, I can see that!" complimented Mr. Stone. "You must like life in the woods and on the lake."

"Indeed they do," spoke Aunt Kate. "They walked—I think it was two hundred miles, just before coming on this cruise; didn't you, Betty?"

"Yes, but we took it by easy stages," evaded the Little Captain.

"That was fine!" exclaimed Mr. Kennedy. "Well, Harry, if we're gong to eat we'd better take our salt and go."

"Won't you have some of our sandwiches?" asked Mollie, impulsive as usual. "We have more than we can eat," for they had brought along a most substantial lunch. Mollie looked at Betty and Aunt Kate. They registered no objections.

"You are very good," protested Mr. Kennedy, "but really we don't want to deprive you——"

"It will be no deprivation," said Betty. "We will be glad not to have them wasted——"

"Oh, then by all means let us be—the wastebaskets!" exclaimed Mr. Stone, laughing.

"Oh, I didn't mean just that," and Betty blushed.

"I understand," he replied, and Aunt Kate passed over a plate of chicken sandwiches. Under cover of opening another bottle of olives, Mollie whispered to Grace:

"Ask him some questions—start on motoring—ask if they ever motored near Deepdale."

"I will," whispered Grace, and, as the two young men ate, she led the topic of talk to automobiles.

"Do you motor?" she asked, looking directly at Mr. Stone. She was certain now that at least he had been in the car that caused Prince to run away.

"Oh, yes, often," he answered. "Do you?"

"No, but I am very fond of horseback riding," she said. She was certain that Mr. Stone started.

"Indeed," said he, "that is something I never cared about. Frankly, I am afraid of horses. I saw one run away once, with a young lady, and——"

"Do you mean that time we were speeding up to get out of the storm?" his friend interrupted, "and we hit a stone, swerved over toward the animal, and nearly struck it?"

"Yes, that was the time," answered Mr. Stone. Grace could hardly refrain from crying out that she was on that same horse.

"I have always wondered who that girl was," Mr. Stone went on, "and some day I mean to go back to the scene of the accident, and see if I can find out. I have an idea she blames us for her horse running away. But it was an accident, pure and simple; wasn't it, Bob?"

"It certainly was. You see it was this way," he explained, and Grace felt sure they would ask her why she was so pale, for the blood had left her cheeks on hearing that the young men were really those she had suspected. "Harry, here, and myself," went on Mr. Kennedy, "had been out for a little run, to transact some business. We were on a country road, and a storm was coming up. We put on speed, because we did not want to get wet, and I had to be at a telegraph office at a certain time to complete a deal by wire.

"Just ahead of us was a girl on a white horse. The animal seemed frightened at the storm, and just as we came racing past our car struck a stone, and was jolted right over toward the animal. I am not sure but what we hit it. Anyhow the horse bolted. The girl looked able to manage it, and as it was absolutely necessary for us to keep on, we did so."

"I looked back, and I thought I saw the horse stumble with the girl," put in Mr. Stone, "but I was not sure, and then the rain came pelting down, and the road was so bad that it took both of us to manage the car. We were late, too. But we meant to go back and see if any accident happened."

"Only when we got to the telegraph office," supplied his friend, "we were at once called to New York in haste, and so many things have come up since that we never got the chance. Tell me," he said earnestly, "you girls live in Deepdale. This happened not far from there. Did you ever hear of a girl on a white horse being seriously hurt?"

Grace made a motion to her chums to keep silent about the whole affair, and let her answer. She had her reasons.

"There was no report of any girl being seriously hurt at the time you mention," she said, a trifle coolly, "but a little child was knocked down by a horse—a white horse. It may have been the one you scared."

"But unintentionally—unintentionally! I hope you believe that!" said Mr. Stone earnestly.

"Oh—yes—of course," and Grace's voice was not quite so cold now. She could readily understand that the accident could have happened in just that way, and it was beginning to look so. Certainly, not knowing the girls, the young man could have no object in deceiving them,

"A little child knocked down, you say!" exclaimed Mr. Kennedy. "I hope it was not badly hurt. Who was it?"

"My——" began Mollie, and she was on the point of saying it was her sister Dodo, when from the lake there sounded the cry of:

"Fire! Fire! Fire!"

Then came a sharp explosion. Everyone arose, and Mr. Kennedy exclaimed excitedly:

"That must be an explosion on a motor boat. Come on, Harry. We may he needed!"

They rushed through the bushes toward the place whence the alarm came, the girls following as fast as they could.

"Don't let him know it was I, or that it was your sister who was hurt!" Grace cautioned her chums. "I am going to write to papa, and he can make an investigation. Their explanation sounds all right, but they may have the papers after all. I'm going to write to-day."

"I would," advised Aunt Kate." "It may amount to nothing, but it can do no harm to let your father know. And I think it wise not to let these young men know that you were in that runaway. If they really were not careless, as it seemed at first, you can tell them later, when you see how the investigation by Mr. Ford turns out."

"That will be best," spoke Betty. "Oh, see, it is a boat on fire!"

They had reached a place where they could see a small motor boat, not far from shore, wrapped in a pall of black smoke, through which could be observed flickering flames.

"There—he's jumped!" cried Mollie, as a figure leaped from the burning craft. "He's safe, anyhow."

"There go Mr. Kennedy and Mr. Stone in their boat!" exclaimed Grace, as the slender racing craft shot out from shore.

Whatever may have been the faults of the young men as motorists, they knew how to act promptly in this case. As they passed the man who had leaped from the burning boat they tossed him a life preserver.

Then, nearing the burning boat, they halted their own, and began using a chemical extinguisher—the only safe thing save sand with which to fight a gasoline blaze. The fire did not have a chance to get much headway, and it was soon out, another boat coming up and lending aid.

The man who had jumped was taken aboard this second boat, and his own, rather charred but not seriously damaged, was towed to shore. Later the girls learned that there had been some gasoline which leaked from his tank. He had been repairing his motor, which had stalled, when a spark from the electric wire set fire to the gasoline. There was a slight explosion, followed by the fire.

"And it came just in time to stop me from telling what might have spoiled your plans, Grace," said Mollie, when they went back to gather up their lunch baskets.

"Well, I haven't any plans. I am going to let father or Will make them, after I send the information," she answered, "But I think it best to let the two young men remain in ignorance, for a while."

"Oh, I do, too!" exclaimed Betty. "They will probably not refer to it again, being so busy over the regatta."

There was a busy time for the girls, too. They finally decided to convert the *Gem*, as nearly as possible under the circumstances, into a Venetian gondola. By building a light wooden framework about it, and tacking on muslin, this could be done without too much labor. Betty engaged the help of a man and boy, and with the girls to aid the work was soon well under way.

The girls saw little of Mr. Kennedy and Mr. Stone—save passing glimpses—after the picnic. Grace telephoned to her father, who promised to at once look into the matter.

"I do hope we win a prize!" exclaimed Mollie, on the evening of the regatta. "The *Gem* looks lovely!"

"Yes, I think it is rather nice," admitted Betty.

The muslin, drawn tightly over the temporary frame, had been painted until in the dark the boat bore a striking resemblance to a gondola, even to the odd prow in front. It was arranged that Grace should stand at the stern with a long oar, or what was to pass for it, while Betty would run the motor and do the real steering. Mollie, Amy, and Aunt Kate were to be passengers. Mollie borrowed a guitar and there was to be music and singing as they took part in the water pageant.

"Well, it's time to start," announced Betty after supper. "We'll light the Chinese lanterns after we get to our place in line," for the boats were to be illuminated.

The *Gem* started off, being in the midst of many craft, all more or less decorated, that were to take part in the affair.

CHAPTER XV

THE RACE

Like the scene from some simulated fairyland, or a stage picture, was the water pageant on Rainbow Lake. In double lines the motor boats moved slowly along from the starting point toward the float where the judges were stationed to decide which craft was entitled to the prize in its own class.

"Oh, I'm so glad we entered!" cried Betty, as she stood at the wheel. Because of the cloth side of the "gondola" it appeared that she was merely reclining at her ease, as did the Venetian ladies of old, for a seat with cushions had been arranged near the steering wheel.

"Oh, see that boat—just like an airship!" exclaimed Mollie, as they saw just ahead of them a craft so decorated.

"And here's one that looks just like a floating island, with trees and bushes," added Amy. "That ought to take a prize."

"We ought to take one ourselves!" exclaimed Mollie. "We worked hard enough. My hands are a mass of blisters."

"And my back aches!" declared Grace. "But it was worth while. I don't see any boat just like ours," and she glanced along the line of craft ahead of them, and to those in the rear, as they were making a turn just then.

"Oh, there's one of the lanterns gone out!" cried Mollie. "I'll light it," and she proceeded to do so, taking it into the cabin because of the little breeze that blew over the lake.

There was a band on one of the larger boats, and this played at intervals.

"Let's sing!" proposed Grace, and, with guitar accompaniment, the girls mingled their voices in one of the many part songs they had practiced at school. Applause followed their rendition, for they had chosen a time when there was comparative quiet.

Around the course went the flotilla of boats, past the judges' float, and back to the starting point. Then the parade was over, but a number of affairs had been arranged—dances, suppers and the like—by different cottagers. The girls had been invited to the dance at the headquarters of the Rainbow Lake Yacht Club, and they had accepted. They had dressed for the affair, and tying their boat to the club dock they went into the pretty little ballroom with Aunt Kate.

"Congratulations!" exclaimed Mr. Kennedy, stepping up to Betty as she entered with her chums.

"For what?"

"Your boat won first prize for those of most original design. It is a beautiful silver cup."

"Oh, I'm so glad! Girls, do you hear? We won first prize in our class!"

"Fine!" cried Mollie.

"Oh, isn't it nice?" said Amy.

"Did we really?" asked Grace, somewhat incredulously,

"You really did. I just heard the decision of the judges. Harry and I are out of it, though. We tried in the 'wreck' class, but the Rabbit, which was rigged out like the Flying Dutchman, beat us."

"That's too bad," said Mollie, sympathetically.

"Never mind, we've had our fun," said Mr. Stone, coming up at this point. "You girls certainly deserved the prize, if anyone did. And now I hope your dance cards aren't filled."

They were not—but they soon were, and the evening passed most delightfully.

"Who said breakfast?" yawned Grace the next morning, as she looked from her bunk down on Betty.

"I ate so much lobster salad last night I don't want anything but a glass of water on toast," murmured Mollie. "Oh, but we had a lovely time!" and she sighed in regret at its departure.

"And those young men were lovely dancers," said Betty.

"And wasn't it nice of Will, Frank, and Allen to come?" spoke Amy, for Grace's brother, and his two friends, had arrived most

91

unexpectedly at the Yacht Club ball. Will had come to tell his sister certain things in regard to the missing papers, and had met a friend who belonged to the club.

Naturally there was an invitation to the dance, which was quite informal in a way, and so the three boys from Deepdale had also had a good time. They were put up at the club over night.

It developed that Mr. Ford had investigated certain matters in regard to Mr. Kennedy and Mr. Stone, and had learned that by no possibility could they have secured the missing papers. There would have been absolutely no interest in the documents for them. It was merely a coincidence that they had been on the scene. And this news made their explanation about the auto accident most plausible.

Will had come to Rainbow Lake to tell his sister this, to relieve her mind. When he mentioned coming he had told Frank and Allen, asking them to go with him. All the boys expected to do was to spend the evening on board the *Gem* with the girls, but when they arrived, and learned of the pageant, and Will met his club friend, the plans were changed.

"Too bad Percy Falconer didn't come," remarked Grace, as she slipped into her dressing gown.

"Don't spoil everything," begged Betty. "You know I detest him!"

Gradually the girls got breakfast, talking of the events of the night before.

"I wonder when we will get our prize?" said Betty. "I am wild to see it. I hope it's that oddly shaped cup we so admired when we looked at the prizes."

It proved to be that one, the trophy being sent over to the dock where the *Gem* was tied, by a special messenger. It was given the place of honor in the cabin.

Will and his two chums went home rather late that day.

"Is father much worried about the missing papers?" asked Grace, as she parted from her brother.

"He sure is. He's afraid the other side may spring something on him any minute."

"You mean—take some action to get the property?"

"Yes."

"It's too bad. But I don't see what we can do."

"Neither do I. I wish I could find Prince. I think that's the queerest thing about him."

"It certainly is. Say, Will, how is poor little Dodo getting on?"

"Oh, as well as you can expect. They're going to operate soon, I heard. How is Mollie standing it, Grace?"

"Fairly well. Isn't it strange that we should meet the two autoists?"

"Yes. Have you put them wise yet?"

"Wise? What do you mean? Such slang!"

"I mean told 'em who you are?"

"No, and we're not going to for a while yet. We don't want to make them feel bad."

"All right, suit yourselves. We're coming up and see you when you get in camp."

"Yes, do. We'll write when we're settled."

Preparations for the race were going on, and the *Gem*, as were the other boats, was being groomed for the contest. She had been converted into her own self again, and Betty had engaged a man to look over the motor, and make a few adjustments of which she was not quite capable.

Uncle Amos came to Rainbow Lake to see the girls and the boat. He was not much impressed with the sheet of water, large as it was, but he did take considerable interest in the coming race, and insisted on personally doing a lot of work to the boat to get her "ship-shape."

So that when the *Gem* was ready to go to the starting line she was prepared to make the "try of her life," as Betty expressed it.

There were six boats in the class that included the *Gem*. Some were about the same size, one was larger and one was smaller. In horse power they rated about the same, but some handicapping had been done by the judges. The *Gem* was to start four minutes after the first boat got away, and of course she would have to make up this time to win.

"But we can do it!" declared Betty, confidently.

As they were on their way to the starting line the girls noticed two boys rowing along the shore, looking intently as they proceeded.

"Say, you haven't seen a big green canoe, with an Indian's head painted in red on each end; have you?" asked one of the lads.

"No; why?" asked Grace.

"Someone took ours last night," spoke the other boy. "We were going in the races with it, too. It was a dandy canoe!" and he seemed much depressed.

"That's too bad," spoke Betty sympathetically. "If we see anything of your canoe we'll let you know."

"Just send word to Tom Cardiff, over at Shaffer's dock!" cried the elder boy eagerly. "There's a reward of two dollars for anyone who finds it."

"Poor fellows!" said Betty as they rowed off. "I'd give two dollars of my own now if we could find their canoe for them. They must be dreadfully disappointed. Well, shall we start?"

"Yes, let's get it over with," replied Grace, nervously.

Grace and Amy were selected to look after the motor, they having been "coached" by Uncle Amos for several days. They were to see that it did not lack for oil, and if anything got out of adjustment they could fix it. They would be stationed well forward in the cabin, and the bulkhead being removed, they could easily get at the machinery.

Betty and Mollie would be at the wheel. Aunt Kate declined to take part in the race, and Uncle Amos was not eligible under the rules, this being strictly a race for girls and women.

94

Several events were run off before the Class B race was called. Then the boats, including the *Gem*, moved up, and were formally inspected to make sure that all the rules and regulations had been complied with. No fault was found.

"Are you all ready?" asked the starter.

"Ready," was the answer, and the first boat shot away. It was nervous waiting for Betty and her chums—those four minutes—but they finally passed.

"Ready?" asked the starter again.

"Ready," answered Betty, her voice trembling in spite of herself. There was a sharp crack of the pistol, and the *Gem* shot ahead, as Betty let the clutch slip into place. The race was on!

CHAPTER XVI

FIGHTING FIRE

"Betty, do you think we can win?"

It was Mollie who asked this as she stood beside her chum at the wheel of the *Gem*. The boat was churning through the water, gradually creeping up on the craft that had gotten away ahead of her. Behind came other boats, starting as the crack of the official pistol was heard.

"Of course we'll win!" exclaimed Betty, as she changed the course slightly. She wanted to keep it as straight as possible, for well she knew that the shortest distance between any two points is in a straight line.

"We wouldn't miss that lovely prize for anything," called Grace from up forward, where she was helping Amy look after the laboring motor.

A number of prizes had been provided by the regatta committee; the chief one for this particular race was a handsome cut-glass bowl, that had been much admired when on exhibition at the club house.

The course was a triangular one of three miles, and now all the craft that were competing were on the last "leg" of the triangle.

"We're creeping up on her!" whispered Amy, as she directed the attention of Grace to the boat just ahead of them. It was a light, open affair, with a two-cylinder motor, but speedy, and two girls in it seemed to be working desperately over their machinery. Something seemed to have gone wrong with one of the cylinders, for Betty could detect a "miss" now and then.

"Yes, we're coming up," admitted Grace, as she skillfully put a little oil on a cam shaft. "If we can only hold out!"

"Oh, trust Betty for that."

"It isn't that—it's the motor. One never knows when they are not going to 'mote.' But this one seems to be coming on well," and Grace glanced critically at the various parts.

They were well out in Rainbow Lake now, and many eyes were watching the race. One of the last boats to get away had given up, for the girls in charge could not remedy the ignition trouble that developed soon after they started. This left five. The *Gem* was second in line, but behind her a very powerful boat was gradually creeping up on her, even as she was overhauling the boat that got away first.

"Can't you turn on a little more gasoline?" asked Mollie.

"I think I can—now," spoke Betty. "I wanted to give it gradually."

She opened the throttle a little more, and advanced the spark slightly. The result was at once apparent. The *Gem* shot ahead, and the girls in the leading boat looked back nervously.

"One of them is that pretty girl Will danced with so often at the ball," said Mollie, as she got a glimpse of the rival's face.

"Yes, and the other is her cousin, or something," spoke Betty. "I was introduced to her. It's mean, perhaps, to beat you, girls," she whispered, "But I'm going to do it."

The chugging of many motors—the churning to foam of the blue waters of the lake—a haze of acrid smoke hanging over all, as some cylinder did not properly digest the gasoline vapor and oil fed to it, but sent it out half consumed—spray thrown up now and then—the distant sound of a band—eager eyes looking toward the stake buoys—tense breathing—all this went to make up the race in which our outdoor girls were taking part.

Foot by foot the *Gem* crept up on the *Bug*, which was the name of the foremost boat. Drop by drop Betty fed more gasoline to her striving motor. The other girls did their duty, if it was only encouragement. Those in the *Bug* worked desperately, but it was not to be. The *Gem* passed them.

"We're sorry!" called Betty, as she flashed by. The other girls smiled bravely.

The *Gem* was now first, but the race was far from won. They were on the last leg, however, but in the rear, coming on, and overhauling Betty and her chums as they had just overhauled the others, was the speedy *Eagle*. She had been last to get off, but had passed all the others.

"They are after us," spoke Mollie, as she held the wheel a moment while Betty tucked under her natty yachting cap some wind-tossed locks of hair.

"But they shan't get us," declared the Little Captain grimly. "We haven't reached our limit yet."

Once more she gave more gasoline, but the rivals in the rear were settling down now to win the race for themselves. The *Eagle* came on rapidly. The finish line was near at hand, but it seemed that Betty and her chums had the upper hand.

Suddenly Grace cried:

"One of the wires is broken. It's snapped in two, and it's spouting sparks!"

There came a noticeable slowing down to the speed of the motor. The *Gem* lagged. The *Eagle* was in hot pursuit. Betty acted quickly.

"Put on those rubber gloves!" she ordered. "Take a pair of pliers, and hold the ends of that wire together. That will make it as good as mended until after the race. Amy, you help. But wear rubber gloves, and then you won't get a shock. Quick, girls!"

The breaking of the wire threw one cylinder out of commission. The *Gem* was one third crippled. There came a murmur from the pursuing boat. There was a commotion in the forward engine compartment of Betty's boat. This was caused by Grace and Amy seeking to repair the damage.

A moment later the resumption of the staccato exhaust of the motor told that the break had been repaired—temporarily, at least. The boat shot ahead again, at her former speed, and only just in time, for her rival was now on even terms with her.

"Oh, Betty, we can't do it!" Mollie said, pathetically. "We're going to lose!"

"We are not! I've got another notch I can slip forward the gasoline throttle, and here it goes! If that doesn't push us ahead nothing will— and — —"

"We don't get that cut glass," finished Mollie.

But just that little fraction was what was needed. The *Gem* went ahead almost by inches only, but it was enough. The *Eagle's* crew of three girls tried in vain to coax another revolution out of her propeller, but it was not to be, and the *Gem* shot over the line a winner. A winner, but by so narrow a margin that the judges conferred a moment before making the announcement. But they finally made it. The *Gem* had undoubtedly won.

"Oh!" exclaimed Grace as she climbed out into the cabin, and thence to the deck, followed by Amy. "Oh, my hand is numb holding the ends of that wire together. I didn't dare let go — —"

"It was brave of you!" exclaimed Betty, patting Grace on the shoulder. "If you had let go we would have lost. We'll bathe your hand for you in witch hazel."

"Oh, it is only cramped. It will be all right in a little while."

"What a din they are making!" cried Amy, covering her ears with her hands.

"They are saluting the winner," said Mollie, as she noted the tooting of many boat whistles. Betty slowed down her boat, and saluted as she swept past the boat of the judges.

"Well, I'm glad it's over," sighed Grace. "It was nervous work. I'm going to make some chocolate, and have it iced. It was warm up there by the motor."

"And you both need baths," remarked Mollie with a laugh. "You are as grimy as chimney sweeps."

"Yes, but we don't mind," said Amy. "You won, Betty! I'm so glad!"

"We won, you mean," corrected the Little Captain. "I couldn't have done it except for you girls,"

Many craft saluted the *Gem* as she came off the course.

"I wish Uncle Amos could have seen us!" exclaimed Betty. "He would have been proud." The girls remained as spectators for the remainder of the carnival, and then, the day being warm, they went to their dock. Near it was a sandy bathing beach, and soon they were swimming about in the limpid waters of Rainbow Lake.

"Here goes for a dive!" cried Mollie, as she climbed out on the end of the pier, and mounted a mooring post. She poised herself gracefully.

"Better not—you don't know how deep it is," cautioned Betty.

"I'm only going to take a shallow dive," was the answer and then Mollie's slender body shot through the air in a graceful curve, and cut down into the water. A second later she bobbed up, shaking her head to rid her eyes of water.

"That was lovely!" cried Grace.

"Did I splash much?"

"Not at all."

"It's real deep there," said Mollie. "Some day I'm going to try to touch bottom."

The girls splashed about, refreshing themselves after the race. Then came calm evening, when they sat on deck and ate supper prepared by Aunt Kate.

"Now you girls just sit right still and enjoy yourselves," she told them, when they insisted on helping. "You don't win motor boat races every day, and you're entitled to a banquet."

That night there was another informal dance at the Yacht Club, and the girls had a splendid time. Mr. Stone and Mr. Kennedy exerted themselves to see that our friends did not lack for partners, and Grace was rather ashamed of the suspicions she had entertained concerning the twain.

The carnival came to an end with a series of water sports. There were swimming races for ladies, and Mollie won one of these, but her chums were less fortunate. The carnival had been a great success and many congratulations were showered on Messrs. Stone and Kennedy for their part in it.

"We are glad it is over," said Mr. Stone, as he and his chums sat on the deck of the *Gem* one evening, having called to ask the girls to go to another dance. But Betty and her chums voted for staying aboard, and proposed a little trip about the lake by moonlight. Soon they were under way.

It was a perfect night, and the mystic gleam of the moon moved them to song as they swept slowly along under the influence of the throttled-down engine.

Suddenly Mr. Kennedy, who was sitting well forward on the trunk cabin with Grace, sprang to his feet, exclaiming:

"What's that?"

"It looks like a fire," said Grace.

"It is a fire!" cried Mr. Stone. "Say, it's that hay barge we noticed coming over this evening, tied up at Black's dock. It's got adrift and caught fire!"

"Look where it's drifting!" exclaimed Betty.

"Right for the Yacht Club boathouse!" added Mollie. "The wind is taking it there. Look, the fire is increasing!"

"And if it runs against the boat house there'll be no saving it!" said Mr. Kennedy. "There's no fire-boat up here—there ought to be!"

"Girls!" cried Betty, "there's just a chance to save the boat house!"

"How?" demanded Amy.

"If we could get on the windward side of that burning barge, throw a line aboard and tow it out into the middle of the lake, it could burn there without doing any damage!"

"By Jove! She's hit the nail on the head!" declared Mr. Stone, with emphasis. "But dare you do it, Miss Nelson?"

"I certainly will dare—if you'll help!"

"Of course we'll help! Steer over there!"

The burning hay, fanned by a brisk wind, was now sending up a pillar of fire and a cloud of smoke. And the barge was drifting perilously near the boathouse. Many whistles of alarm smote the air, but no boat was as near as the *Gem*.

CHAPTER XVII

ON ELM ISLAND

"Have you a long rope aboard, Miss Nelson?" asked Mr. Stone, when they had drawn near to the burning load of hay.

"Yes, you will find it in one of the after lockers," answered Betty, as she skillfully directed the course of her boat so as to get on the windward side of the barge.

"And have you a boathook? I want to fasten it to the rope, and see if I can cast it aboard the barge."

"There is something better than that," went on the Little Captain. "I have a small anchor—a kedge, I think my Uncle Amos called it."

"Fine, that will be just the thing to cast! Where is it?"

"In the same locker with the rope. Uncle insisted that I carry it, though we've never used it."

"Well, it will come in mighty handy now," declared Mr. Kennedy, as he prepared to assist his chum. "You girls had better get in the cabin," he added, "for there is no telling when the wind may shift, and blow sparks on your dresses. They're too nice to have holes burned in them," and he gazed, not without proper admiration, at Betty and her chums. Even in this hour of stress and no little danger he could do that.

"We'll put on our raincoats," suggested Mollie. "The little sparks from the hay won't burn them. Or, if they do, we can have a pail of water ready."

"That's a good idea," commented Mr. Stone, who was making the kedge anchor fast to the long rope. "Have several pails ready if you can. No telling when the sparks may come aboard too fast for us."

"And we have fire extinguishers, too," said Betty. "Grace, you know where they are in the cabin. Get them out."

"And I'll draw the water," said Mr. Kennedy.

"I can help at that," added Aunt Kate, bravely. "I know where the scrubbing pail is." She had insisted on making it one of her duties to scrub the deck every day, and for this purpose she kept in readiness a pail to which a rope was attached, that it might be dropped overboard into the lake and hauled up full. This was soon in use. Aunt Kate insisted on having several large pots and pans also filled.

"You can't have too much water at a fire," she said, practically.

The burning hay barge was rapidly being blown down toward the boathouse. At the latter structure quite a throng of club members, and others, had gathered in readiness to act when the time came.

In the moonlight they could be seen getting pails and tubs of water in readiness, and one small line of hose, used to water the lawn, was laid. But it would be of small service against such a blaze as now enveloped the barge. Many boats were hastening to the scene, whistling frantically—as though that helped.

"Have you got a pump aboard?" some one hailed those on the *Gem*.

"No, we're going to haul the barge away," answered Betty.

"Good idea, but don't go too close!" came the warning.

"It is going to be pretty warm," remarked Mr. Stone. He had the anchor made fast, and with the rope coiled so that it would not foul as he made the cast, he took his place on one of the after lockers. Betty's plan was to go as close to the burning craft as she could, to allow the cast to be made, As soon as the prongs of the anchor caught, she would head her motor and out toward the middle of the lake, towing the barge where it could be anchored and allowed to burn to the water's edge.

"But what are you going to anchor it with?" asked Mr. Kennedy, when this last feature had been discussed.

"That's so," spoke his chum, reflectively.

"There's a heavy piece of iron under the middle board of the cabin," said Betty. "Uncle Amos said it was there for ballast in case we wanted to use a sail, but I don't see that we need it."

"We'll use it temporarily, anyhow, for an anchor," decided Mr. Stone. He and his companion soon had it out, and made fast to the other end of the rope.

"Get ready now!" warned Betty, when this had been done. "I'm going as close as I can."

She steered her boat toward the burning barge. There came whistles of encouragement from the surrounding craft. The heat was intense, and on the suggestion of Mr. Kennedy the motor boat's decks were kept wet from the water in the pails. The girls felt their hands and faces grow warm. Those on the boathouse float and pier were all anxiety. The flames, blown by the wind, seemed to leap across the intervening space as if to reach the boat shelter.

"Here she goes!" cried Mr. Stone, as he cast the anchor. It was skillfully done, and the prongs caught on some part of the barge, low enough down so that the hempen strands would not burn. Mr. Stone pulled on the rope to see if it would hold. It did, and he called:

"Let her go, Miss Nelson! Gradually though; don't put too much strain on the rope at first! After you get the barge started the other way, it will be all right."

Betty sent the *Gem* ahead. The rope paid out over the stern—taunted—became tight. There was a heavy strain on it. Would it hold? It did, and slowly the hay barge began to move out into the lake.

"Hurray!" cried Mr. Kennedy. "That solved the problem."

"You girls certainly know how to do things," said Mr. Stone, admiringly.

Cheers from those in surrounding boats seemed to emphasize this sentiment. There was now no danger to the Yacht Club boathouse.

A little later, when the flames in the hay were at their height, the piece of iron was dropped overboard from the *Gem*. This, with the rope and the kedge anchor, served to hold the barge in place. There it could burn without doing any harm.

Soon the fire began to die down, and a little later it was but a smouldering mass, not even interesting as a spectacle. Betty Nelson's plan had worked well, and later she received the thanks of the Yacht Club, she and her chums being elected honorary life members in recognition of the service they had rendered.

Summer days passed—delicious, lazy summer days—during which the girls motored, canoed or rowed as they fancied, went on picnics in the woods, or on some of the islands of Rainbow Lake, or took long walks. Mr. Stone and Mr. Kennedy, sometimes one, often both, went with the girls. Occasionally Will and his friends ran out for a day or two, taking cruises with Betty, and her chums.

Aunt Kate remained as chaperone, others who had been invited finding it impossible to come. The girls' mothers made up a party and paid them a visit one day, being royally entertained at the time.

"Yes, you girls certainly know how to do things," said Mr. Stone one day; after Betty had skillfully avoided a collision, due to the carelessness of another skipper.

"I wish we could do something to get those papers for father," thought Grace. Not a trace had been found of Prince or the missing documents. It was very strange. Mr. Ford and his lawyer friends could not understand it. The interests opposed to him were preparing to take action, it was rumored, and if the papers were found this would be stopped. Even a detective agency that made a specialty of tracing lost articles had no success. Prince and the papers seemed to have vanished into thin air.

One day as Betty and her chums were motoring about the lake, having gone to the store for some supplies, they saw the two boys who had been searching for their canoe.

"Did you find it?" asked Grace.

"No, not a trace of it, Too, bad, too, for we saved up our money— four dollars, now," said the taller of the two lads. "If you find her we'll give you that money; won't we?" and he appealed to his companion.

"We sure will!"

"Well, if we see, or hear, anything of it we'll let you know," promised Betty. "Poor fellows," she murmured, as they rowed away.

They had made a circuit of the lake, going in many coves, but without success.

"It's about time to be thinking of camp, if we're going in for that sort of thing," announced Betty one day. "Shall we try it, girl?"

"I'd like it," said Mollie. "We can use the boat, too; can't we?"

"Of course," replied Betty.

"And sleep aboard?" asked Grace.

"No, let's sleep in a tent," proposed Amy. "It will be lots of fun."

"But the bugs, and mosquitoes—not to mention frogs and snakes," came protestingly from Grace.

"Oh, we've done it before, and we can use our mosquito nets," said Betty. "I heard of a nice tent, and a well-fitted up camp over on Elm Island we can hire for a week or so."

"But the ghost—the one Mr. Lagg told about?" asked Mollie.

"We'll 'lay' the ghost!" laughed Betty. "Seriously, I don't believe there is anything more than a fisherman's story to account for it. Still, if you girls are afraid——"

"Afraid!" they protested in chorus.

"Then we'll go to Elm Island," decided Betty, and they did. The camp, near a little dock where the *Gem* could be tied, was well suited to their needs.

"Oh, we'll have a good time here!" declared Betty as they took possession. "But we must get in plenty of supplies. Let's go over and call on Mr. Lagg," and they headed for the mainland in the motor boat.

CHAPTER XVIII

IN CAMP

"Well, well, young ladies, I certainly am glad to see you again! Indeed I am."

"Ladies, ladies, one and all,

I'm very glad to have you call!"

Thus Mr. Lagg made our friends welcome as they entered his "emporium," as the sign over the door had it.

"What will it be to-day?" he went on.

"I've prunes and peaches, pies and pills,

To feed you well, and cure your ills."

"Thank you, but we haven't any ills!" cried "Brown Betty," as her friends were beginning to call her, for certainly she was tanned most becomingly. "However, we do want the lottest lot of things. Where is that list, Mollie?"

"You have it."

"No, I gave it to you."

"Grace had it last," volunteered Amy. "She said she did not want to forget— —"

"Oh, we know what Grace doesn't want to forget," interrupted Mollie with a laugh. "Produce that list, Grace," and it was forthcoming.

"You see we have let our supplies run low," remarked Betty as she gave her order,

"Are you going on a long cruise?" Mr. Lagg, wanted to know.

"To sail and sail the bounding main,

And then come back to port again?

"Of course I know that isn't very good," he apologized. "When I make 'em up on the spur of the moment that way I don't take time to polish 'em off. And of course Rainbow Lake isn't exactly the bounding main, but it will answer as well."

"Certainly," agreed Betty, with a laugh. "I think that is all," she went on, looking at her list. "Oh, I almost forgot, we want some more of your lovely olives—those large ones."

"Yes, those are fine olives," admitted the store keeper. "I get them from New York.

"Olives stuffed, and some with pits,

 With girls my olives sure make hits."

He chanted this with a bow and a smile.

"I am aware," he said, "I am aware that the foregoing may sound like a baseball game, but such is not my intention. I use hit in the sense of meaning that it is well-liked."

"Too well liked—I mean the olives," spoke Mollie. "We can't keep enough on hand. I think we'll have to buy them by the case after this."

"As Grace does her chocolates," remarked Betty, with a smile that took all the sarcasm out of the words.

"Well," remarked Grace, drawlingly, "I have noticed that you girls are generally around when I open a fresh box."

"Well hit!" cried Amy. "Don't let them fuss you, Grace my dear."

"I don't intend to."

Mr. Lagg helped his red-haired boy of all work to carry the girls' purchases down to the boat.

"You must be fixing for a long voyage," he remarked.

"No, we are going to camp over on Elm Island," said Betty.

The storekeeper started.

"What! With the ghost?" He nearly dropped a package of fresh eggs.

"Really, Mr. Lagg, is there—er—anything really there?" asked Mollie, seriously.

"Well, now, far be it from me to cause you young ladies any alarm," said Mr. Lagg, "but I only repeat what I heard. There is something on that island that none of the men or boys who have seen and heard it cannot account for."

"Just what is it?" asked Betty,

"Do you want me to tell you?"

"Certainly—we are not afraid. Though we mustn't let Aunt Kate know," said Betty, quickly.

"Well, it's white and it rattles," said Mr. Lagg.

"Sounds like a riddle," commented Amy. "Let's see who can guess the answer."

"White—and rattles," murmured Betty. "I have it—it's a pan full of white dishes. Some lone camper goes down to wash his dishes in the lake every night, and that accounts for it."

"Then we'll ask the lone camper—to scamper!" cried Grace with a laugh. "We want peace and quietness."

"And you are really going to camp on Elm Island?" asked Mr. Lagg, as he put the purchases aboard.

"We are," said Betty, solenmly. "And if you hear us call for help in the middle of the night——"

"Betty Nelson!" protested Amy.

"And if for help you call on I—

I'll come exceeding quick and spry!"

Thus spouted Mr. Lagg.

"I am painfully aware," he said, quickly, "that my poem on this occasion needs much polishing, but I sometimes make them that way, just to show what can be done—on the spur of the moment. Howsomever, I wish you luck. And if you do need help, just holler, or light a fire on shore, or fire a gun. I can see you or hear you from the end of my dock." Indeed, Elm Island was in sight.

The girls went back with their supplies, and soon were in camp. The hard part of the work had been done for them by those of whom they had hired the tent and the outfit. All that remained to do was to light the patent oil stove, and cook. They could prepare their meals aboard the boat if they desired, and take them to the dining tent. In short they could take their choice of many methods of out-door life.

Their supplies were put away, the camp gotten in "ship-shape," cots were made up, and mosquito bars suspended to insure a night of comfort. A little tour was made of the island in the vicinity of the camp, and, as far as the girls could see, occasional picnic parties were the only visitors. There were no other campers there.

"We'll have a marshmallow roast to-night," decided Betty, as evening came on. They had gathered wood for a fire on the shore of the lake, and the candy had been provided by Grace, as might have been guessed.

"I hope the ghost doesn't come and want some," murmured Mollie.

"Hush!" exclaimed Betty. A noise in the woods made them all jump. Then they laughed, as a bird flew out.

"Our nerves are not what they should be," said Betty. "We must calm down. I wonder did we get any pickles?"

"I saw him put some in," spoke Grace.

"Then let's have supper, and we'll go out for a ride on the lake afterward," suggested Betty.

"Maybe the ghost will carry off our camp," remarked Amy.

"Don't you dare let Aunt Kate hear you say that or she'll run away!" cried Betty. "Come on, everyone help get supper, and we'll be through early," and, gaily humming she began to set the table that stood under a canvas shelter in front of the big tent.

CHAPTER XIX

A QUEER DISTURBANCE

"Have we blankets enough?"

"It's sure to be cool before morning."

"We can burn the oil stove turned down love—that will make the tent warm."

"Oh, but it makes it so close and—er—smelly."

They all laughed at that.

Betty and her chums were preparing to spend their first night in camp on Elm Island, in the tent. They had had supper—eating with fine appetites—and after a little run about the lake had tied up at the small dock near their tent.

"A lantern would be a good thing to burn," said Aunt Kate. "That will give some warmth, too."

"And we can see better, if—if anything comes!" exclaimed Amy, evidently with an effort.

"Anything—what do you mean?" demanded Mollie, as she combed out her long hair, preparatory to braiding it.

"Well, I mean—er—*anything*!" and again Amy faltered.

"Oh, girls she means—the ghost!" exclaimed Betty, with a laugh. "Why not say it?"

"Don't!" pleaded Grace.

"Now look here," went on practical Betty. "There's no use evading this matter. There's no such thing as a ghost, of that we are certain, and yet if we shy at mentioning it all the while it will only make us more nervous."

"The idea! I'm not nervous a bit," declared Mollie.

"Well, then," resumed Betty, "there's no use in being afraid to use the word, as Amy seemed to be. So talk ghost all you like—you can't scare me. I'm so tired I know I'll sleep soundly, and I hope the rest of you will. Only, for goodness sakes, don't be talking in weird whispers. That is far worse than all the ghosts in creation."

"That's what I say!" exclaimed Aunt Kate, who was an old-fashioned, motherly soul. "If the ghost comes I'm going to talk to it, and ask how things are—er—on the other side. Girls, it's a great privilege to have a ghostly friend. If the man who owns this island knew what was good for him he'd advertise the fact that it was haunted. If Mr. Lagg were here I'd get him to make up a poem about the ghost. That would scare it off, if anything could."

"That's the way to talk!" cried Betty, cheerfully. "And now for a good night's rest. Bur—r—r—r! It *is* cold!" and she shivered.

"I'm going to get some more blankets from the boat," declared Mollie. "I know we'll be glad of them before morning. Come along with me, Grace," she added, after a moment's pause, as she took up one of the lanterns. "You can help carry them."

"And scare away the——" began Amy.

"Indeed, I wasn't thinking a thing about it!" insisted Mollie, with emphasis. "And I'll thank you to——"

She began in that impetuous style, that usually presaged a burst of temper, and Betty looked distressed. But Mollie corrected her fault almost before she had committed it.

"Excuse me, Amy," she said, contritely. "I know what you mean. Will you come, Grace?"

"Of course. I'll be glad of some extra coverings myself."

The two girls were back in remarkably short time.

"You didn't stay long," commented Betty, drily. "it's only a step to the dock," answered Mollie, as she and Grace deposited their arm-loads of blankets on the cots.

Then after the talk and laughter had died away, quiet gradually settled down in the camp tent. The Outdoor Girls were trying to go to sleep, but one and all, afterward, even Aunt Kate, complained that it was difficult. Whether it was the change from the boat, or the talk of the ghost, none could say. At any rate there were uneasy turnings from side to side, and as each cot squeaked in a different key, and as one or the other was constantly "singing," the result may be imagined.

"Oh, dear!" exclaimed Grace, impatiently, after a half-hour of comparative quiet, "I know I'll never get to sleep. Do you girls mind if I sit up and read a little? That always makes me drowsy, and I've got a book that needs finishing." Only Aunt Kate was slumbering.

"Got any chocolates that need eating?" asked Mollie, with a laugh, in which they all joined, half-hysterically.

"Yes, I have!" with emphasis. "But, just for that you won't get any."

"I don't want them! You couldn't hire me to eat candy at night," and again Mollie flared up.

"Girls, girls!" besought Betty. "This will never do! We will all be rags in the morning."

"Polishing rags then, I hope," murmured Amy. "My hands are black from the oil stove—it smoked, and I'll need a cake of sand-soap to get clean again."

"Well, I can't stand this—I'm too fidgety!" declared Grace. "I'm going to sit up a little while, and read. I'm going to eat a chocolate, too. I'll give you some, Mollie, if you like. I bought a fresh box of Mr. Lagg.

"Chocolates they are nice and sweet,

Good for man and beast to eat."

"Give me a young lady-like brand," suggested Amy.

"Why don't we all of us sit up a while, and—I have it—we'll make a pot of chocolate," exclaimed Mollie. "That will make us all sleep, and warm us—it is getting real chilly already."

"Perhaps that will be best," agreed Betty, as she donned her heavy dressing gown and warm slippers, for the tent was cool even in July.

Soon there was the aroma of chocolate in the little cooking shelter, and the girls sat around, in various picturesque and comfortable attitudes, sipping the warm beverage and nibbling the crisp crackers.

Then gradually their nerves quieted down, and even Grace, more aroused than any of the others, began to feel drowsy. One by one they again sought their cots, and finally a series of deep breathings told of much-needed sleep.

It must have been long after midnight when Betty was suddenly aroused by a queer noise. She had slept heavily, and at first she was not fully aware of her surroundings, nor what had awakened her. Then she became conscious of a curious heavy breathing, as of some animal. She sat up in alarm, her heart pounding furiously. Her throat went dry.

"Girls—girls!" she gasped, hoarsely. "Aunt Kate!"

The latter was the first to reply. Quickly reaching out to the lantern near her, she turned up the wick. Following the sudden illumination in the tent there was a cracking in the underbrush near it.

"Oh!" screamed Grace, sitting up. "What is it?"

"I'm going to look!" said Mollie, resolutely.

"Don't! Don't!" pleaded Amy, but Mollie was already at the flap of the tent, which she quickly loosed. Then she screamed.

"Look! It's white! It's white!"

Betty, forcing herself to action, stood beside her chum. She was just in time to see some-thing big and white run down toward the lake. There was a clash and jingling as of chains, and a splashing of water. Then the white thing disappeared, and the girls stood staring at one another, trembling violently.

CHAPTER XX

THE STORM

Grace "draped" herself over the nearest cot. Amy followed her example, with the added distinction that she covered her head with the blankets. Betty and Mollie stood clinging to each other.

"Though I don't think they were any braver than we," declared Grace afterward. "They simply couldn't fall down, for Betty wanted to go one way and Grace the other. So they just naturally held each other up."

"I couldn't stand," declared Amy. "My, knees shook so."

Aunt Kate was the first to speak after the apparition had passed away, seeming to lose itself in the lake.

"Girls, have you any idea what it was?" she asked.

"The—the—" began Amy. "Oh, I can't say it!" she wailed from beneath the covers.

"Don't be silly!" commanded Betty, sharply. "If you mean—ghost—say so," but she herself hesitated over the word.

"If that was the ghost it was the queerest one I ever saw!" declared Mollie, with resolution. "I don't just mean that, either," she hastened to add, "for I never saw a ghost before. But in all the stories I ever read ghosts were tall and thin, of the willowy type——"

"Like Grace," put in Betty, with rather a wan smile.

"Don't you dare compare me to a ghost!" commanded the Gibson girl," with energy that brought the blood to her pale cheeks. She ventured to peer out from under the tent flap now. "Is it—is it gone?" she faltered.

"It's in the lake—whatever it was," said Mollie. "But wasn't it oddly shaped, Betty?"

"It was indeed. And it made plenty of noise. Real ghosts never do that."

"Oh, some do!" asserted Amy. "I read the 'Ghost of the Stone Castle,' a most fascinating story, and that ghost always rattled chains, and made a terrible noise."

"What did it turn out to be?" asked Aunt Kate.

"The story didn't say. No one ever found out."

"Well, this one is exactly like Mr. Lagg described," spoke Grace, "chains and all. What could it have been?"

"I imagine," said Betty, slowly, "that it may be some wild animal——"

Grace screamed.

"What is it now?" asked Betty, regarding her.

"Don't say wild animals—they're worse than ghosts!"

"Nonsense! Don't be silly! I mean it may he some wild animal, like a fox or deer that has been caught in a trap. Traps have chains on them, you know. This animal may have been caught some time ago, have pulled the chain loose, and the poor thing may be going around with the trap still fastened to him. That would account for the rattling."

"Yes," said Mollie, "that may be so, and there may be white foxes, but I never heard of any outside of Arctic regions. But, Betty Nelson, there never was a fox as large as that. Why it was as—as big as our tent!"

"Yes, and how it sniffed and breathed!" added Betty. "I guess it couldn't be a wild animal. It may have been a cow. I wonder if any campers here keep a white cow?"

"A cow would moo," declared Grace.

"But whatever it was, it was frightened at the light," said Aunt Kate, practically, "so I don't think we need to be afraid of it—whatever it was. We'll leave a light outside the tent the rest of the night, and it won't come back."

"I'm going to sleep in the boat!" declared Grace.

"Nonsense!" cried Betty. "Don't be a deserter! Have some more chocolate, and we'll all go to sleep," and they finally persuaded Grace to remain. It took some little time to get their nerves quiet, but finally they all fell into a more or less uneasy slumber that lasted until morning. The "ghost" did not return.

Wan, and with rather dark circles under their eyes, the girls got breakfast the next morning. The meal put them in better spirits, and when they bustled around about the camp duties they, forgot their scare of the night before.

They made a partial tour of the island, though some parts were too densely wooded and swampy to penetrate. But such parts as they visited showed the presence of no other campers. They were alone on Elm Island, save for an occasional picnic party, several evidently having been there the day before.

"Then that—thing—couldn't have been a cow," said Grace, positively.

"Make up a new theory," suggested Betty, with a laugh. "One thing, though, we're not going to let it drive us away, are we—not away from our camp?"

The others did not answer for a moment, and then Mollie exclaimed:

"I'm going to stay—for one."

"So am I!" declared Aunt Kate, vigorously. "A light will keep whatever animal it is away, and I'm sure it was that. Of course we'll stay!"

There was nothing for Grace and Amy to do but give in—which they did, rather timidly, be it confessed.

"And now let's go for a ride," proposed Betty, after lunch. "There are some things I want to get at Mr. Lagg's store."

"Will you tell him about the—ghost?" asked Grace.

"Certainly not. It may be," said Betty, "that some one is playing a joke on us. In that case we'll not give him the satisfaction of knowing that we saw anything. We will keep silent, girls." And they did.

"Matches, soap and oil and butter,

Business gives me such a flutter."

Mr. Lagg recited this as Betty gave her order.

"Have you seen the ghost?" he asked.

"Oh!" cried Grace, "you have in some fresh chocolates! I must have some."

"You'll find my chocolates sweet and good,

To eat on lake or in the wood!"

Mr. Lagg's attention being diverted to a net subject, he did not press his question. Thus the girls escaped committing themselves.

"I think we are going to have a storm," remarked Betty, when they were under way again, cruising down the lake toward Triangle Island, where they expected to call on some friends. "And as Rainbow gets rough very quickly, I think we shall turn back."

"Yes, do," urged Amy. "I detest getting wet."

"The cabin is dry," urged Grace.

"We had better go back," urged Aunt Kate, and the prow of the *Gem* was swung around. Other boats, too small or not staunch enough to weather the blow that was evidently preparing, had turned about for a run to shore. There passed Betty's craft the two boys whose canoe had been taken.

"Any luck?" asked Betty, interestedly.

"No, we haven't found a trace of it yet," the older one replied.

In the West dark masses of vapor were piling up, and now and then the clouds were split by a jagged chain of lightning, while the ever-in-creasing rumble of thunder told of the onrush of the storm.

"We're going to get caught!" declared Mollie. "I guess I'll close the ports, Betty."

"Do; and bring out my raincoat, please."

Attired in this protective garment over her sailor suit, the Little Captain stood at the wheel.

With a blast that flecked the crests of the waves into foam, with a rattle and roar, and a vicious swish of rain, the storm broke over the *Gem* while she was yet a mile from the camp on Elm Island. The boat heeled over, for her cabin was high and offered a broad surface to the wind.

"We'll capsize!" screamed Amy.

"We will not!" exclaimed Betty, above the noise. She shifted the wheel to bring the boat head-on to the waves, and this made her ride on a more even keel. Then, with a downpour, accompanied by terrific thunder and vivid lightning, the storm broke. Betty bravely stood to her post, the others offering to relieve her, but she would not give up the wheel, and remained there until the little dock was reached. Then, making snug their craft, they raced for the tent. It had stood up well, for it was protected from the gale by big elm trees. Soon they were in shelter.

And then, almost as suddenly as it had come up, the storm passed. The clouds seemed to melt away, and the sun came out, the shower passing to the East.

Grace, who had gone out on the end of the dock, called to the others.

"Oh, come on and see it!"

"What—the ghost?" inquired Mollie.

"No, but the most beautiful rainbow I ever saw—a double one!"

They came beside her, and Grace pointed to where, arching the heavens, were two bows of many colors, one low down, vivid and perfect, the other above it—a fainter reflection. As the sun came out from behind the clouds the colors grew brighter.

"How lovely!" murmured Amy, clasping her hands.

"Yes, it is the most brilliant bow I have ever seen," added Aunt Kate. "It seems almost like like a painted one." I would be more poetical if I were Mr. Lagg," and she laughed.

"It is very vivid," went on Betty. "In fact I have heard it said that on account of the peculiar situation of this lake, the high mountains around it, and the clouds, there are brighter rainbows here than anywhere else in this country. That is how the lake got its name—Rainbow. It was the Indians who first gave it that, I was told, though I don't know the Indian name for rainbow."

"We don't need to—this is beautiful as it is," murmured Grace. "Oh, isn't it wonderful!" and they stood there admiring the beautiful scene, and recalling the old story of the bow—the promise of the Creator after the flood that never again would the world be submerged.

Then the light gradually died from the colored arches, to be repeated again in the wonderful cloud effects at sunset. The storm had been like the weeping of a little child, who smiles before its tears—and afterward.

CHAPTER XXI

THE GHOST

"Girls, there are letters for each of us!" exclaimed Betty.

"Any for me?" asked Aunt Kate.

"Yes, a nice—adipose—that is to say, fleshy one," exclaimed Mollie, passing it over. It was bulky.

The girls had stopped at the store of Mr. Lagg, where they had sent word to have their mail forwarded. The occasion was a morning visit several days after they had established their camp on Elm Island.

"Any news?" asked Betty of Mollie, the former having finished a brief note from home, stating that all were well.

"Yes, poor little Dodo is to go to the specialist to be operated on this week. Oh, it does seem as if I ought to go home, and yet mamma writes that I am to stay and enjoy myself. She says there is practically no danger, and that there is great hope of success. Aunt Kittie— Dodo was at her house when the accident happened, you know— Aunt Kittie has come to stay with mamma. Every one else is well, including Paul.

"Oh, but I shall be so anxious until it is over! They are going to let me know as soon as it is. Are we going to stay around here, where I can get word quickly?"

"Yes, we will remain on Elm Island, I think," said Betty. "There is no use in cruising about too much when we are so comfortable there, and really it is lovely in the woods."

"As long as the ghost doesn't bother us," spoke Amy.

"Nonsense!" exclaimed Betty. "What is your news, Grace?"

"Oh, Will writes that he and Frank are coming up to camp on the island near us."

"That will be fine!" exclaimed Betty. "When will they get here?"

"Allen can't come up until the week-end," went on Grace. "He has to take some kind of bar examinations. For the—high jump, I think."

"Silly!" reproved Betty, with a blush.

"But Will told me to tell you specially that Allen is coming," went on Grace. "They can stay a few days."

"It will be fine," cried Mollie. "Any news about the papers, Grace?"

"Not a word, and no trace of Prince."

"That is queer," said Betty. "But we will live in hopes—that Dodo will be all right, and that the papers will be found."

"Indeed we will," sighed Grace. Mr. Lagg was bowing and smiling behind his counter while the girls were reading their letters.

"What will it be? What will it be? What will it be to-day?

 Be pleased to leave an order, before you go away!"

"Really, I don't believe we need a thing," answered Mollie, in answer to this poetical effusion. "We might have——"

"Some more olives," interrupted Grace. "They are so handy to eat, if you wake up in the night, and can't sleep."

"Shades of Morpheus preserve us!" laughed Mollie. "Olives!"

"Does the ghost keep you awake?" asked the storekeeper.

"Not—not lately!" answered Betty, truthfully.

"The ghost! The ghost! with clanking chains,

 It comes out only when—it rains!"

Thus Amy anticipated Mr. Lagg.

"Very good—very good!" he commended. "I must write that down. Hank Lefferton was over setting eel pots on the island last night, and he said he seen it."

"The ghost?" faltered Betty.

"Yep. Chains and all."

"Well, we didn't," said Aunt Kate, decidedly. "Come along, girls."

They had written some souvenir cards, which they mailed, and again they went sailing about Rainbow Lake.

123

Several days passed. The girls went on little trips, on picnics, cruised about and spent delightful hours in the woods. They thoroughly enjoyed the camp, and the "ghost" did not annoy them. Mollie waited anxiously for news from home, but none came.

Then the boys arrived, with their camping paraphernalia, and in such bubbling good spirits that the girls were infected with them, for they had become rather lonesome of late.

The boys pitched their tent near that of the girls, and many meals were eaten in common. Then one night it happened!

It was late, and after a jolly session—a marshmallow roast, to be exact—they had all retired. No one remained awake now, for the girls had become used to their surroundings, and the boys—Allen included, for he had come up—were sound sleepers.

There was a crash of underbrush, a series of snorts—no other word describes them—and the screaming girls, hastening to their tent flaps, cried:

"The ghost! The ghost!"

"Get after it, fellows!" called Will, as he recognized his sister's voice. "We'll lay this chap—whoever he is!"

There was a vision of something white, again that rattling of chains, and a plunge into the lake. Then all was still.

CHAPTER XXII

WHAT MOLLIE FOUND

"Did you get—it?"

Betty hesitated a moment over the question.

Will, Frank and Allen stood just outside the tent of the girls. They had come back from a hurried race after the white object that had again disturbed the slumbers of the campers.

"We only had a glimpse of it," answered Will. "Then it seemed to melt into the water."

"But it was big," said Frank.

"And made lots of noise," added Allen.

"That's just the way it acted before," declared Mollie.

In dressing gowns, warmly wrapped up, and in slippers, the girls were talking through the opened flap of the tent to Grace's brother and his chums.

"Can you imagine what it may be?" asked Aunt Kate. She had been making chocolate—a seemingly never-failing remedy for night alarms.

"Haven't the least idea," answered Will, "unless it's someone trying to play a so-called practical joke."

"I'd like to get hold of the player," announced Allen. "I'd run him off——"

"Off the scale," interrupted Betty, with a laugh.

"That's it," conceded Allen. "Are you girls all right?"

"All but our nerves," answered Grace.

The boys made a search in the gloom, but found nothing, and once more quiet settled down. Nor were they disturbed again that night. In the morning they laughed.

"Oh, but it's hot!" exclaimed Mollie during the forenoon, when the question of dinner was being discussed. "I think we might go for a swim. There's a nice sandy beach at the side of our dock."

"Let's!" proposed Grace. The boys had gone off fishing.

Soon the girls were splashing around in the lake, making a pretty picture in their becoming bathing suits, of which they had more use than they had anticipated.

"Let's try some diving!" proposed Mollie, always a daring water sprite. "It's lovely and deep here," and she looked down from the end of the dock.

"I wish I dared dive," said Amy. She was a rather timid swimmer, slow and deliberate, probably able to keep afloat for a long time, but always timid in deep water.

"Here goes!" cried impulsive Mollie, as she poised for a flash into the water.

She went down cleanly, but was rather long coming up. Grace and Betty looked anxiously at one another.

"She is— —" began Betty.

Mollie flashed into sight like a seal.

"I—I found something!" she panted.

"Did you strike bottom?" asked Betty.

"Almost. But that's all right. I'm going down again. There is something down there. Maybe it's the ghost!"

"Oh, do be careful!" cautioned Betty, but Mollie was already in the water. She was longer this time coming up, and Betty was getting nervous. Then Mollie shot into view.

"I—I found it!" she gasped.

"What?" chorused the others.

"The missing canoe those boys have been looking for! It is down there on the bottom, freighted with stones. We will get it up for them!"

CHAPTER XXIII

SETTING A TRAP

"Are you sure it is the canoe?" asked Betty, who did not want Mollie to take any unnecessary risks.

"Of course I am," came the confident answer, as Mollie poised, in her dripping bathing suit, on the little dock. She made a pretty picture, too, with her red cap, and blue suit trimmed with white. "I could feel the edge of the gunwhale," she went on, "and the stones in it that keep it down."

"But how can we get it up?" asked Grace, who was sitting on the dock, splashing her feet in the water. Grace never did care much about getting wet. Amy said she thought she looked better dry. Certainly she was a pretty girl and knew how to "pose" to make the most of her charms—small blame to her, though, for she was unconscious of it.

"We can get it up easily enough," declared Mollie, wringing the water from her skirt, "All we'll have to do will be to toss out the stones, one by one, and the canoe will almost float itself. I can tie a rope to the bow, and we can stand on shore and pull. Those boys will be so glad to get it back."

"But can we lift out the heavy stones?" asked Amy, in considerable doubt.

"Of course we can. You know any object is much lighter in water than out of it, we learned that in physics class, you remember. The water buoys it up. You can move a much heavier stone under water than you could if the same stone was on land. We can all try."

"I never could stay under water long enough to get out even one stone," declared Grace.

"Nor I," added Amy.

"I'll try," spoke Betty—she was always willing to try—"but I'm afraid I can't be of much help, Mollie. And I'm sure I don't want you to do it all."

"Well, wait until I make another inspection," said the diving girl. "It may be more than I bargained for. I'll hold my breath longer this time."

"Do be careful!" cautioned Aunt Kate, coming out from the tent.

"We will," promised Betty.

Again Mollie dived. She had practiced the trick of opening her eyes under water, and this time she looked carefully over the sunken canoe. She stayed under her full limit, and when she came up she was panting for breath.

"You must not stay under so long," warned Betty.

"There—are—a—lot—of—stones," gasped Mollie. "But I think we can do it," she added a moment later.

"I'll see what I can do," spoke Betty. She was a good swimmer and diver, perhaps not so brilliant a performer as Mollie, but with more staying qualities. Down went Betty in a clean dive, and when she came up, panting and shaking the water from her eyes, she called:

"I lifted out two, but I think we had better let the boys do it, Mollie."

"Perhaps," was the reply.

"I'm sorry you can't count on me," sail Grace, "but really I'd have nervous prostration if I went down there, even though it's only ten feet deep, as you say."

"Well, getting nervous prostration under water would be a very bad idea," commented Betty.

"And I'm sure I never could do it," remarked Amy. "Do let the boys manage it, Bet. The lads who own the canoe will be glad of the chance."

"I'm going to move out a couple of stones, so Betty won't beat my record," laughed Mollie, diving again. She bobbed up a moment later.

"Oh, dear!" she cried. "An eel slid right over me. Ugh! I'm not going down again!" and she shivered. Even the fearless Mollie had had enough of the under-water work.

By means of a cord and a float the position of the sunken canoe was marked, so that the boys could locate it, and when they returned from a rather unsuccessful fishing trip, they readily agreed to raise the boat. It did not take them long to remove the stones, for Will, Frank and Allen were all expert swimmers, and could remain under water much longer than can most persons.

Then a rope was made fast to the canoe, which would not rise completely because of being filled with water. It was pulled ashore and word sent to the young owners. That they were delighted goes without saying. They proffered the reward they had offered, but of course our friends would not take it. Later it was learned that the canoe had been taken by an unscrupulous fisherman, who was not above the suspicion of making a practice of such tricks. It was thought he intended to let it remain where it was until fall, when he would raise it, paint it a different color, and sell it. But Mollie's fortunate dive frustrated his plans.

"Seen anything more of the ghost?" asked Will of the girls, when the canoe had been moored to the shore.

"No, and we don't want to," returned Betty.

"Afraid?" Allen wanted to know.

"Indeed not!" she exclaimed, with a blush.

"I'll tell you what let's do," suggested Frank. "Let's take a look around and see if that ghost left any footprints."

"Ghosts never do," asserted Will.

"Well, let's have a look anyhow. We should have done it before. Now, as nearly as I can recollect, the creature came about to here, and then rushed into the lake," and Frank went to a spot some distance from the tents. The others agreed that it was about there that the white object had been seen. Will was looking along the ground, going toward the lake. Suddenly he uttered an exclamation.

"Girls! Fellows!" he cried. "Come here!" They all hastened to his side. He pointed to some marks in the sandy soil.

"What are they?" he asked, excitedly.

"Hoof marks!" cried Allen, dramatically.

"That's right!" agreed Will. "They are the marks of a horse! Girls, that's what your ghost is—a white horse, and—and——"

He ceased abruptly, looked at Grace strangely, and then brother and sister gasped together:

"Prince!"

"What?" demanded Allen.

"I'll wager almost anything that this ghost is my white horse, Prince, that has been missing so long!" went on Will. "But how in the world he could have gotten on this island, so far from the mainland, is a mystery!"

"Couldn't he swim?" asked Frank.

"Of course!" cried Will. "I forgot about that. And Prince was once a circus horse, or at least in some show where he had to jump into a tank of water. Prince is a regular hippopotamus when it comes to water. Strange I never thought of that before!

"But this solves the ghost mystery, girls. You and the other folks have been frightened by white Prince scooting about the island."

"We—we weren't so very frightened," spoke Mollie.

"But the rattling chains?" questioned Grace.

"What were they?"

"The stirrups, of course," answered her brother. "And, by Jove, Grace, if the stirrups are on Prince the saddle must be on him also, and the papers——"

"Oh, isn't this just fine!" cried Grace, her face alight. "Now papa can complete that business deal. I never loved a ghost before. Dear old Prince!"

"Of course we are assuming a lot," said Will. "It may not be Prince after all, but all signs point to it. He must have been on this island all the while. No wonder we could get no trace of him. Probably he was so frightened at the storm and the auto, and his fall, that he ran on until he came to the lake. Then his old training came back to him, and in he plunged. There's enough fodder here for a dozen horses. He's just been running wild. I'll have my own troubles with him when I get him back."

"But how are you going to do it?" asked Frank.

"We'll search the island for him," replied Will. "Come on, we'll start now."

Changing from their bathing suits to more conventional garments, the boys and girls at once began a tour of the island. But though it was not very large, there were inaccessible places, and it must have been in one of these that Prince hid during the day, for they neither saw, nor heard anything of him.

"We've got to set a trap!" exclaimed Will.

"How?" asked Grace.

"Well, evidently he's been in the habit of coming around the tent to get scraps of food. We'll leave plenty out to-night, and also some oats. Then we'll watch, and when Prince comes I'll catch him."

The boys voted this plan a good one. They went over to Mr. Lagg's store in the *Gem* to get a supply of fodder for the trap.

"A horse on the island!" exclaimed Mr. Lagg. So that's the ghost; eh? Well, it's very likely, but it sort of spoils the story;

"A ghostly ghost—a ghost in white

Appearing in the darkest night.

That it should prove a horse to be,

Most certainly amazes me."

"Good!" exclaimed Will, with a laugh. "You are progressing, Mr. Lagg."

A goodly supply of oats was placed in a box near the tent that evening, and then the boys and girls sat about the camp-fire and talked, while waiting for the time to retire. The boys were to make the attempt to capture Prince.

CHAPTER XXIV

THE GHOST CAUGHT

"When do you expect to hear about little Dodo?" asked Grace, as the girls sat together on a log in front of the fire, "like roosting chickens," Will was ungallant enough to remark.

"Almost any day now," replied Mollie. "They were to wait for the most favorable time for the operation, and the specialist, so mamma wrote, could not exactly fix on the day. But I am anxious to hear."

"I should think you would be. Poor little Dodo! I'd give anything to hear her say now 'Has oo dot any tandy?'"

"Don't," spoke Betty in a low tone to Grace, for she saw the tears in Mollie's eyes.

"It was the strangest thing how Stone and Kennedy should turn out to be the two chaps in the auto," remarked Will, to change the subject. "And you have never let on that Grace was the girl on the horse?"

"Never," answered Amy. "Don't say after this that girls can't keep a secret."

Frank was to watch the first part of the night, to be relieved by Allen, and the latter by Will.

"For, from what the girls say, Prince has been in the habit of coming rather late," Will explained, "and he's more likely to let me catch him than if you fellows tried it. So I'll take last watch."

Frank's vigil was unrewarded, and when he awakened Allen, who sat up, sleepy-eyed, there was nothing to report. Allen found it hard work to keep awake, but managed to do so by drinking cold coffee.

"Anything doing, old man?" asked Will, as, yawning, he got on some of the clothes he had discarded, the more comfortably to lie down on the cot.

"Something came snooping around about an hour ago. At first I thought it was the horse, and went out to take a look. But it was only a fox, I guess, for it scampered away in the bushes. I hope you have better luck."

"So do I. Dad wants those papers the worst way. If I could get them for him I'd feel better, for I can't get over blaming myself that it was my fault they were lost. It was, because I shouldn't have sent Grace for them when I knew how important they were."

Allen went to his cot, and Will took up his vigil. For an hour he sat reading by a shaded lantern, so the light would not shine in the faces of his chums. Then, when he was beginning to nod, in spite of the attractions of the book, he heard a noise that brought him bolt upright in the chair.

"Something is coming!" he whispered. He stole to the edge of the board platform, and cautiously opened the flap of the tent. The box containing oats and sugar had been placed a little distance away, in plain view.

"That's Prince!" exclaimed Will, for in the moonlight he saw a white horse eating from the box. The "ghost" had arrived.

Will resolved to make the attempt alone. He stepped softly from the tent, and made his way toward the horse. He had on a pair of tennis shoes that made his footsteps practically noiseless. Fortunately, Prince, should it prove to be that animal, stood sideways to the tent, his head away from it, so that he did not see Will. The boy tried to ascertain if there was a saddle on the horse, but there was the shadow of a tree across the middle of his back, and it was impossible to say for sure.

Nearer and nearer stole Will. He thought he was going to have no trouble catching him, but when almost beside Prince, for Will was certain of the identity now, he stepped on a twig, that broke with a snap.

With a snort Prince threw up his head and wheeled about. He saw Will, and leaped away.

"Prince, old fellow! Prince! don't you know me?" called the boy, and he gave a whistle that Prince always answered.

The horse retreated. Will held out some sugar he had ready for such an emergency.

"Prince! Prince!" he called. The horse stopped and stretched out his head, sniping. Prank and Allen came to the tent opening. "Keep back!" called Will, in even tones. "I think I have him. Prince! Come here!"

The horse took a step forward. He sensed his master now. Will advanced, speaking gently, and a moment later Prince, with a joyful whinny, was nibbling at the sugar in the boy's hand. Then Will slid the other along and caught the mane. The bridle was gone.

"I have him!" cried Will. "Bring the rope, fellows."

Prince was not frightened now. He stood still. Will led him into the full moonlight. Then he exclaimed:

"The saddle is gone!"

CHAPTER XXV

THE MISSING SADDLE

"Have you caught Prince?" Grace called this to her brother from the tent where she and the other girls had been aroused by the commotion.

"Yes, I have him. He knew me almost at once," answered Will. "But the saddle is gone!"

"And the papers?" Grace faltered.

"Gone with it, I fancy. Too bad!"

"Maybe he just brushed the saddle off," suggested Allen, who, with Frank, had come out with a rope halter that had been provided in case the "ghost hunt" was a success. "We'll look around. I'll get a lantern."

But a hasty search in the darkness revealed nothing. There was no sign of a saddle.

"We'll have to wait until morning," sighed Will, as he tied Prince to a tree. "Then we can see better, and look all around. Prince, old boy, you knew me; didn't you?" The handsome animal whinnied, and rubbed his nose against Will's arm.

"And so you played the part of a ghost, you rascal! Scaring the girls— —"

"We'll never admit that," called Betty from the tent.

There was nothing more to do that night, after making Prince secure. The boys ate a little mid-night supper, and from the tent of the girls came the odor of chocolate, which Grace insisted on making. Then, after fitful slumbers, morning came.

Will was up early to examine Prince. He found the healed cut, where the auto had struck, and there was evidence that the saddle had been on the animal until recently. The iron stirrups would account for the sound like chains.

"The saddle must be somewhere on this island," declared Will. "I'm going to find it."

"How?" asked Allen, who had made a careful toilet, as Betty had promised to go for a row with him.

"I'll strap a pad on Prince, get on his back, and see where he takes me. The way I figure is this. Prince never liked to be in the open. I'm almost certain he has been staying in some sort of shelter—either a cave, or an old cabin, or stable on the island. The saddle may have come off there. Now he'll most likely take me right to his stopping place. Of course he may not, but it's worth trying."

"Indeed it is," agreed Prank.

After a hasty breakfast Will put his plan to the test. Prince was fed well, and with Frank and Allen to follow, Will leaped on his pet's back, and gave him free rein—or, rather, free halter, since there was no bridle. The girls said they would take a walk around the island, looking for the saddle as they went.

Prince, after a little hesitation, started off with Will on his back. The splendid animal headed for the lake shore, and for a moment Will was inclined to think that Prince was going to plunge in and swim to some other island or the mainland. But Prince was only thirsty, and, slaking that desire, he ambled along the shore for a mile or so, the two young men following.

"Where can he be going?" asked Frank.

"Just let him alone," counseled Will. "He knows what he is about."

And so Prince did. He took a path he had evidently traveled many times before, to judge by the hoof-marks, and presently came to a swampy place at which Frank and Allen balked.

"Wait here," advised Will. "I'll soon be back. This is near one end of the island. It must be here that Prince has his stable."

And so it proved. Splashing through the swamp, Prince ascended a little slope, pushed under some low tree branches that nearly brushed Will from his back, and came to a halt before a tumbled-down cabin, that was just about large enough for an improvised stable. Will leaped off, gave a look inside, and uttered a shout of joy, for there, trampled on and torn, broken and water-stained, was the saddle. A second later Will was kneeling before it, exploring the saddle pockets.

"Here they are!" he cried, as he pulled out the missing papers. "I have them, fellows!"

A hasty survey showed him that they were all there—somewhat stained and torn, to be sure, but as good as ever for the purpose intended.

"This is great luck!" cried Will. He looked about him. Then he saw the reason why Prince had made this place his headquarters. The former occupant of the deserted cabin had left behind a quantity of salt, and as all animals like, and need, this crystal, Prince had been attracted to the place. It was like the old "buffalo licks." Then, too, there was shelter from storms.

"Prince, old man, you're all right!" cried Will, as he put the papers in his pockets. By dint of a little hasty repairing the saddle could be used temporarily. It was evident that Prince had kept it on until lately, and the dangling stirrups had caused the sound like rattling chains. There was no sign of the bridle, however, but the halter would answer. Will saddled his pet, and soon had rejoined Frank and Allen, to whom he had shouted the good news. Then a hasty trip was made back to camp.

"Oh, I'm so glad!" cried Grace. "Now I can really enjoy camping and cruising. You must telephone papa at once."

Which Will did, the whole party going over to Mr. Lagg's store in the motor boat.

"Yes, I have the papers safe," Will told Mr. Ford. "Yes, I'll mail them at once. What's that—Dodo—tell Mollie Dodo is over the operation and is going to get well? I will—that's good news! Hurrah!"

"Oh, thank the dear Lord!" murmured Mollie, and then she sobbed on Betty's shoulder.

"Well, I guess we are ready to start," announced Grace. "I have the chocolates. Who has the olives?"

"Chocolates and olives—the school girl's delight!" mocked Will,

"Oh, you'll be asking for some," declared his sister.

"Chocolates and olives are good for the boys,

And to the girls they also bring joys."

Thus remarked Mr. Lagg. The crowd of young people were in his store, stocking up the *Gem* for a resumption of her cruise on Rainbow Lake. It was several days after the finding of the missing saddle and the papers. The latter had been sent to Mr. Ford, Prince had been swum across to the mainland and sent home, and the news about little Dodo had been confirmed. The child would fully recover, and not even be lame.

"Oh, what a fine time we've had!" exclaimed Grace, as she waltzed about the store with Amy.

"Well, the summer isn't over yet by any means," spoke Mollie. "And there is the glorious Fall to come. I wonder what we shall do then?"

And what they did do may be ascertained by reading the next volume of this series, to be called "The Outdoor Girls in a Motor Car; Or, The Haunted Mansion of Shadow Valley," in which we will meet all our old friends again, and some new ones.

"All aboard!" called Betty, as she led the way down to the dock where the *Gem* awaited them. Each one was carrying a bundle of supplies, for they expected to cruise for about a week.

They boarded the motor boat. Betty threw over the lever of the self-starter. The engine responded promptly. As the clutch slipped in, white foam showed at the stern where the industrious propeller whirled about. The *Gem* slid away from the dock.

"Good-bye! Good-bye!" called the boys and girls to Mr. Lagg.

"Good-bye!" he answered, waving his red handkerchief at them. Then he recited.

"As you sail o'er the bounding sea,

Pause now and then and think of me.

I've many things for man and beast,

From chocolate drops to compressed yeast."

"Good!" shouted Will, laughing.

And Betty swung around the wheel to avoid the two boys whose canoe Mollie had so strangely found, as the *Gem*, continued her cruise down Rainbow Lake. And here, for a time, we, too, like Mr. Lagg, will say farewell to our friends.

THE END

CPSIA information can be obtained
at www.ICGtesting.com
Printed in the USA
LVHW012309260721
693792LV00002B/147

9 781006 719509